INSANITY 3

CIRCUS

by Cameron Jace

www.CameronJace.com

Copyright

First Original Edition, December 2015

Other Books by Cameron Jace

The Grimm Diaries Prequels Series

The Grimm Diaries Prequels 1-6 (Free)

The Grimm Diaries Prequels 7-10

The Grimm Diaries Prequels 11-14

The Grimm Diaries Prequels 15-18

The Grimm Diaries Main Series

Snow White Sorrow (book 1)

Cinderella Dressed in Ashes (book 2)

Blood, Milk & Chocolate Part 1 (book3)

I Am Alive Series

I Am Alive (book 1)

Pentimento Series

Pentimento (book 1)

Books in the Insanity Series

Insanity

Figment

Circus

Hookah (coming soon

How to read this book:

Begin at the beginning
and go until you come to the end;
then stop.

For those mad enough to believe in themselves, in spite of what the world says.

Prologue Part One

The Six O'clock Circus, Mudfog Town, London

Saturday, 11:41 p.m.

The man with the rabbit stood in the middle of the circus while the children and their parents waited with anticipation. This was it! The Maddest Show on Earth, performed by the one and only magician who called himself the Hatter.

The man wore a top hat. It was black, elegant, and rather funny. Several teaspoons and watches were neatly wrapped around the rims. He was tall. Almost seven feet. And he wore ridiculously tall boots with silver pins and stars. The hat made him look even *taller*.

The children liked him. He was different, mysterious, and not as boring as their parents. Maddeningly funny, although he rarely spoke.

But what the children absolutely loved about him were his goggles, which made him look like a huge bee. A crooked nose beaked out from underneath the goggles. Not an assuring sight for the parents at first. But the children still liked it. They knew it was meant to be silly, nonsensical, and absurd. Things the older folks rarely understood. Besides, it probably wasn't the Hatter's real nose.

The Hatter had a double chin, so strong it squeezed an old shilling between its cheeks. Not once had he dropped it, as if it were glued.

He wore a tuxedo. It made him look a bit mature, compared to the absurdness of his face, hat, and goggles. But not really. It was a black tux, with spoons for buttons, sugar cup buttons for his sleeves, and teabags dangling from his upper pockets instead of a rose or a napkin.

The children, who had been coming every week for almost two months, also liked his glittering gold pocket watch. They knew the time on that watch was always six o'clock.

Always.

That was why the Hatter claimed he never aged. Also why he never grew hungry. More significant, it was why he had his sugar cups and spoons always ready. He had to always have his six o'clock tea, which in his case was all day long.

The Maddest Show on Earth always started at six o'clock.

It also ended at six o'clock.

Any time in between was, you guessed it, six o'clock.

Usually the parents would curse the watchmakers on their way out of the circus each night, whining about their malfunctioning watches while inside the circus.

The children would snicker, winking at each other. They knew the Hatter could stop time. But no parent would have believed them.

Right now, almost midnight in the outside world, six o'clock inside the circus, the show was about to begin.

Prologue Part Two

The Six O'clock Circus, Mudfog Town, London

Saturday, 11:51 p.m.

Today, in a small, almost abandoned circus at the outskirts of London, the Hatter had promised the kids the Maddest Trick of All Time. It included a rabbit.

But there was no rabbit to be seen. Not yet.

The Hatter took off his hat, a few teacups plummeting to the sandy floor of the dimly lit circus. Without saying a word, he waved the hat in the air.

Silence sucked off the breathing air. Everyone watched with anticipation.

The Hatter slowly approached the circle's rim, showing the hat to the audience. It was empty. He summoned a couple of kids to show them the hat, allowing them to confirm it was empty. Then he made them sit back next to their parents, who had paid nothing for this show. The Maddest Show on Earth was for free.

Then the Hatter pulled out something that worried the parents, but made the children's eyes widen with excitement. It was a *bomb*, full of colorful wires wrapped around a digital screen.

The Hatter's lips twitched. He seemed worried too. The bomb could blow up any minute. The parents squinted, grimaced, and tensed. The children, well, they were about to merrily clap their hands.

Accidentally, the Hatter, posing like a magician, pushed a button on the wired bomb.

It began ticking.

A few parents shrieked, holding their children tighter.

"It's just a show, Mum!"

"Be a man, Dad!"

The timer ticked on a countdown from 666. Hours? Minutes? Seconds? No one knew.

"Tick..." the Hatter finally said. He placed one hand behind his ears, waiting for the children's response.

"Tock!" The children raised their hands.

"Tick!" The Hatter addressed the crowd on the other side of the circle.

"Tock!" the children screamed. Their parents laughing uneasily.

"That's right," the Hatter said, and sipped from a cup of tea in a nearby table. "Now, what would you say if I told you that no one can stop this bomb?"

The children clapped their hands on their mouths, their eyes almost going kaleidoscopic. The parents were utterly confused. Was this part of the nonsensical show?

"No one but a girl named Mary Ann," the Hatter explained.

"Where is Mary Ann?" the children wailed, or played along to a silly joke. The parents didn't know.

"Mary Ann's gone mad. She can't come and save you." He pouted. "But don't worry." He waved his hand again. "The

Hatter is here to save the day."

"Yay!" The children relaxed.

"You know what I'm going to do with this ticking bomb?" he said.

The children shook their heads.

"I'm going to put it in my hat"—he did—"and wear my hat again." He did that, too.

"But the bomb will explode on your head!" a child offered, his friends laughing.

"Not if I use my magic and turn it to something else." The Hatter smiled.

The children got the message and yelled, "A rabbit."

The Hatter nodded, took off his hat, and pulled out a white rabbit.

The children in the circus clapped, most of them standing up and chuckling. The parents clapped along, still skeptical and worried.

"So the bomb will not explode?" a child asked.

"Hmm..." The Hatter sighed, but said nothing. He let the white, cute rabbit hop toward the crowd. "There are small slices of carrot underneath each of your chairs." He pointed. "It would be nice if you feed it, right?"

The children began competing on attracting the rabbit closer, having picked up the small pieces of carrot. The rabbit was really cute. A bit fat, though. It had bulging and pleading eyes that would have softened the greatest Wonderland

Monster's heart.

Suddenly, amidst the circus's cheering crowd, the rabbit hiccupped.

"Easy on the rabbit," a parent advised. "You're feeding it too much."

But the children realized that this wasn't the case.

Each time the rabbit hiccupped, its ears glowed red. As protective as the parents were, they weren't the first to realize what was going on. It was the children who noticed that each time the rabbit hiccupped, it also ticked.

Slowly, and disappointedly, they raised their heads, looking at the Hatter, who sat sipping tea in the middle of the ring. "I guess the magic trick didn't work." He shrugged. "Try this." He sipped again. "Tick?" He placed a hand behind his ear.

"Tock?" the children said reluctantly, unsure of what kind of game this had turned into.

"Boom!" the Hatter cheered, plowed the teacup against one of the poles that held the circus erect, and waved both hands sideways.

That was when everyone began running like crazy.

All but the Hatter. He stood up and clapped frantically at his own prank. He watched the crowd scream their way out of the circus while a white rabbit with a ticking bomb inside followed, heading to spread terror all over London.

The Hatter pulled out his phone and dialed a number. He dialed 666, then flipped the phone upside down so it dialed 999 by itself. Some magic phone.

"Hello," he said, adjusting his hat. "There is a rabbit loose on the streets of London."

"A rabbit?" the emergency operator at the end of the line said. She almost hung up.

"A rabbit with a bomb in it," the Hatter said. "Don't feed it carrots, or it will hiccup. And, oh, I almost forgot. Only one girl can stop the bomb. Her name is Mary Ann."

Chapter 1

Psychiatry, Radcliffe Lunatic Asylum, Oxford

Sunday, 6:00 a.m.

The mysterious psychiatrist, hiding behind a curtain of darkness, still tries to persuade me of confessing my madness. I lie helpless on the couch, not caring to stand up. How can I when I am crippled all over again?

This situation has begun occurring too often now. About once every three days. I wake up and I am in this darkened room, crippled and listening to the boring lessons from that nutcase on his rocking chair beside me. Sometimes I doubt he is a real psychiatrist—if any of this is even real. Why won't he show his face?

But I have to play along. At least until this episode of hallucination—or whatever is really going on—passes.

It usually takes about ten minutes or so. Then I'd be back in my cell. Sleep for a while, then wake up as if nothing ever happened. I am starting to get used to it, only today's episode started a bit too early. Who examines their patients at six in the morning?

"I see you have a lot of bruises," the psychiatrist says. "Got into a fight lately?"

"I've been practicing."

"Practicing how to stomp against the walls of your cell?"

"No." I sigh. "It's called None Fu."

"Excuse me?"

"None Fu. An abbreviation for Nothing Fu. Like Kung Fu, you know?"

"Kung means 'achievement' or 'work,'" he notes. "Are you saying you're practicing an art that is about 'nothing'?"

"You wouldn't understand." I sigh again, wishing the Pillar would send for me. I am hungry for another mad adventure, longing to save somebody's life. It's the only way I can stay relatively sane.

"Try me."

"It's an art that assumes that all kinds of real training is just bonkers," I say. "Karate, wrestling, and martial arts don't really need laws. Laws only imprison a person's mind, and deprive him from the gift to be free. What you need is 'True Will.'" I read about it in Jack's book.

"Just that?"

"Just that." I nod, aware of the absurdity of my words. "All you need is to 'believe' something is possible to get it done, although believing itself isn't an easy matter."

"So you say you can fight, defend yourself, by mere belief, without having to take a scientific approach or having trained properly?" His voice is flat. I can't tell if he is mocking me or considering it.

"Yes."

"Apparently you didn't learn much." Now he sounds like he's mocking me. "I mean, all those bruises on your body. Did you really hit the walls with your bare hands and feet, like Waltraud informed me?"

"Yes," I say. "It's part of the training. I should be repeating it until mastery." My whole body aches. I have been practicing all week in my cell. Jumping, running against the wall, and walking on my hands. I was following all the nonsensical instructions from the book.

"Mastery?" He smokes that pipe again. I can smell the weirdly familiar tobacco.

"Don't make fun of me," I say. "You're my doctor. You're supposed to help me."

"I *am* helping you," he insists, "by pushing your imagination so hard that your mind can't accept the madness you're imagining anymore. When we reach that tipping point, you'll find yourself remembering, and accepting your reality."

"Which is?" I shrug.

"That you're a troubled girl who killed her friends by driving a school bus into a horrible accident, and that now you're crippled, locked in an asylum because your mind refuses to admit the truth." He blurts the sentence in one breath. "It's a very simple truth, actually. Once you're able to confront it, you'll recover."

I have nothing to say. It scares me to even think about it. Is that all there is to my life? Am I just a mad Alice, thrown down into an imaginary rabbit hole, and now all I need is to confess it was all a dream, just like in Lewis Carroll's book?

"Alice?" He sounds as if trying to gently wake me up from a nightmare.

"Yes, I'm listening," I reply. "You said you're pushing my imagination to the limits until I won't be able to imagine anymore. Right? And that only then will I be forced to retreat back to reality. Is that how you treat all your patients? Because I don't think I've ever heard about this."

"It's a scientific process." His rocking chair creaks against the floor. "We call it the Rabbit Hole."

"You're kidding me, right?"

"No. It's a scientific technique," he says. "The Rabbit Hole is a metaphor for the road you have to fall onto to push your imagination to the max, which will eventually result in igniting a certain suppressed memory or emotion. A memory so real and strong the patient can't deny it. Thus the patient comes back to the real world, and is cured from their madness. Of course, it's coined after Lewis Carroll's book."

I wonder why Lewis Carroll's name comes up in this conversation. Why would a physician coin a scientific method after a man who wrote a children's book? "Trust me, doctor," I say, "I would love it if your method works." I don't know if I am lying. In all honesty, I am beginning to like my own world. The Pillar, the Cheshire, Tom Truckle, the Queen, Fabiola, and Jack. All the madness and nonsense and uncertainty seem to have had a magical impact on me.

"I certainly hope so," he says. "How about I call Waltraud

to roll you back to your cell? We've had enough for today."

"One more thing, doctor," I say. "There is something I'd like to ask you before I go."

"Please do."

"How come physicians are referencing Lewis Carroll in terms like the Rabbit Hole? I mean, isn't Lewis Carroll just a Victorian writer who wrote a children's book?"

"Interesting question. Well, Lewis Carroll had an uncanny interest in mental illness."

"He did?"

"Of course. It's documented," he says. "Also, Lewis himself suffered from terrible migraines, which presumably caused his stuttering. Sometime the migraines left him unconscious for hours, probably dreaming his stories."

"What?" I knew Lewis stuttered. I saw it myself. But I didn't realize he had such horrible migraines.

"He took so many drugs for the migraines, but they wouldn't go away," the doctor elaborates. "He tried to cure himself with the most horrible torture instruments."

"What are you saying, exactly?" I am angered.

"Maybe Lewis Carroll was just as insane," he says, "as you are."

Chapter 2

The Six O'clock Circus, Mudfog Town, London

Sunday, 8:05 a.m.

An hour later, the Pillar's chauffeur drops me off at the so-called crime scene.

It's seven thirty in the morning on a foggy Sunday. After my psychiatry session, I fainted to the sight of my crippled self in the mirror. When I awoke, I wasn't crippled anymore. Waltraud informed me I would be transported to "outside counseling" again. This time, my ruthless warden had looked highly suspicious of the matter, but she couldn't intervene.

The chauffeur picked me up from the asylum's entrance. All through the drive, in the ambulance he still drove from my last adventure, from Oxford to the outskirts of London, he said nothing useful, just that the Pillar had called for me.

A new Wonderland Monster seemed to have arrived.

The rest of the ride I watched the chauffeur drive recklessly and comb his thin whiskers while listening to both his ambulance's siren and the "White Rabbit" song by Jefferson Airplane from the radio. Eventually, I looked away and continued bandaging the wounds on my arms. When will I ever learn this None Fu thing?

Now, I am standing in front of an old circus with a single red, white, and black tent. The circus, if you could call it that, is surrounded with gravel and sand from all sides. No houses or buildings are in sight. The police are everywhere, looking into some crime. I really don't know what I am doing here.

"Take this." The chauffeur pulls out a fake card and hands it over.

"Amy Watson?" I read, furrowing my brow. "Director's assistant at the White Rabbit Animal Rights Movement in London?"

"Pin it to your jacket," the chauffeur demands without explaining. "You'll need it to get past the police."

"What should I actually look for once I get past them?"

"Your boss, Professor *Cornelius Petmaster*, of course." The chauffeur rubs his whiskers. "The one and only." he winks.

Standing in my place, I watch him drive away recklessly, like a spoiled rich kid with his daddy's new ambulance.

Now I have the police's full attention.

"Alice—I mean Amy Watson." I point at my card and approach them confidently, waving my magic umbrella in the other hand. "White Rabbit Animal Rights Movement." I have no idea what I am saying.

"You're looking for Professor Petmaster, I presume." A young, chubby officer sighs, hands on her belt.

I nod.

"Why are those guys even on the crime scene?" She points at me and scowls at another officer. "This is a *crime scene*. What is an animal rights organization doing here?"

"Crime scene?" a tall, overly thin officer says. His flirting eyes are all over me already. He is cute, but lanky, like a flipping broom. Strangely, I fidget. Am I favoring a stranger's random interest in me in the absence of Jack? "You can't call it a crime scene without a body. Besides, a rabbit is on the loose. I know most people care for the bomb. Still, some care for the rabbit. Come in, Ms. Amy." He flashes his teeth at me. That fake grin I notice most boys use to impress girls. I don't have time for this. I shouldn't have any interest in boys. I don't know what the heck is going on.

Averting my eyes, I spot the Pillar a few strides away from the circus's tent. He is pretending he is a music maestro to a few kids who seem to have been in the circus when whatever crime took place. He is singing, "*London Bridge is falling down. Falling down.*" The children reply enthusiastically, "*Down down down!*"

"A very handsome young fellow." A ninety-year-old grandmother winks at me, hands clapped together, pointing at the Pillar.

"I'm sure he is," I mumble. *Young fellow?* I fight the urge to roll my eyes. Everyone seems to like the Pillar wherever I go. If they only knew what a fruitcake he is.

I approach him and the children.

"Watson!" The Pillar welcomes me with his usual theatrical gestures, as if it's the happiest day of his life.

"Professor Petmaster." I nod, hands behind my back, playing my part. Calling me "Watson" reminds me of Sherlock

Holmes. I don't know if it's intentional on the Pillar's behalf, although we do have some similarities in the way we solve cases, and the Pillar does smoke a lot, like Sherlock. "What do we have here?" I ask, hoping I'll finally understand the situation.

"A white rabbit on the loose." He excuses himself from the kids and their parents. "You know how much my heart aches for a stray animal," he says, his voice loud enough so everyone hears. "Poor white rabbit, thrown out in the cruel world of humanity." He pulls me toward the circus, as I spread my fake smiles at the police, parents, and the kids.

"Sorry you caught me singing that awful song," he whispers as we walk in.

"Sorry? Why?"

"Who in the world sings 'London Bridge is falling down' for young kids?" he says. "Such a depressing song."

I try to overlook the interesting fact as we finally enter the circus.

The circus inside is a dirt hole. Cheap as it gets. I glimpse a sign announcing that entrance is for free. I am not surprised. The circus is a bit too dim inside. The ring in the middle is filled with white sand, but empty otherwise. Actually, the whole place is abandoned. A huge flyer dangling from above says "The Maddest Show on Earth." This does seem like a Wonderland Monster's crime scene so far.

"So what happened in here?" I ask the Pillar, now that we're alone, and we can drop the act.

"A man calling himself the Hatter has been performing here for the last month, for free," the Pillar says, walking slowly with his cane and inspecting the place. Dressed the way he is, I realize the Pillar would easily fit in here, mistaken for one of the circus's performers. An insane ringmaster, maybe. "Last night, the so-called Hatter performed a magic trick where he managed to magically make a white rabbit swallow a time bomb."

"Oh." I remember last week's killer stuffing heads in watermelons. I wonder what's with all that stuffing. "And?"

"He showed it to the children. The children panicked and ran away, so did the white rabbit, now loose on the streets of London, hopping happily, waiting to explode." The Pillar seems interested in the sand on the floor inside the ring.

"What's with all the cruelty Wonderland Monsters have toward animals?"

"Almost everyone in Carroll's book *is* an animal, Alice," the Pillar remarks. "I'm one, if you haven't noticed."

Of course, he's not an animal. Or is he?

"So that's why there is no corpse. We're supposed to chase a loose rabbit with a bomb this time?" I change the subject. What, and who, the Pillar is isn't something I want to delve into now. I am just happy to be out there, using my legs and away from the asylum.

"Could be."

"Some kind of wicked Wonderland Monster terrorism attack?"

"I assume so." The Pillar is still fascinated by the ring.

"Why do you seem to have doubts about all of this?" I say. "A bomb inside a rabbit is meant to brutally explode somewhere in London. I can't see it any other way."

"If I'm a terrorist with a bomb, I'd let it just explode wherever I want it to explode." The Pillar squints, still staring at the ring in the middle. "Why let a rabbit loose? Whoever this Wonderland Monster is, he has a mysterious plan I can't put my finger on."

Chapter 3

Sunday, 8:24 a.m.

When I think about it, the Pillar's assumption makes sense. A rabbit with a bomb, let alone how unethical it is, might be meant to stir panic all over the city for a reason or another. I try to figure out what's going on, but I know very little about the situation. "Are you saying this is meant for me and you again, a message from a Wonderland Monster?"

"It's hard to tell. The Wonderland Monsters work in nonsensical ways." The Pillar stops before the ring, not willing to step inside for some reason. What's so important about the sand inside?

"At least we know he is the Mad Hatter this time."

"That's who he claims to be." The Pillar kneels down, thoroughly inspecting the empty ring. "Still, something isn't quite right here."

"The sand?"

The Pillar nods and stands up again. "But I'm not sure yet." He looks at me, as if he is seeing me for the first time. "What's up with all your bruises? Had a fight with Waltraud?"

"Nah, it's None Fu." I swallow the word. "I was training."

"Does it say to try to kill yourself and stick a carrot in your behind in the book?"

"Of course not! There are certain moves, similar to karate, that are supposed to work, but I end up falling on my hips or hitting the wall." I try to sound casual but I am utterly embarrassed. Even to the Pillar, this None Fu thing seems off the rocker. "I'll have to keep doing this until it works."

"You know only insane people do the same thing over and over again, expecting the same results, *over and over again*, right?"

"What's so wrong with insane people?" A half-smile surfaces on my lips.

"Nothing." The Pillar smiles. "They can do whatever they want... and that is the fun of it."

Suddenly, a noise interrupts us.

Someone is snoring in the tiers behind me. I turn around and see a man in his fifties, sitting with his neck resting on his shoulder. He is wearing a long brown duster, and is sleeping on the bank in the highest row in the back. I turn back and shoot the Pillar an inquisitive look.

"Nothing to worry about. That's Chief Inspector Dormouse," the Pillar says. "Sherlock Dormouse." He raises one eyebrow and shields his mouth with one gloved hand.

"You're kidding, right?" I follow the Pillar as he climbs up toward the sleeping inspector.

"I'm not *kidding*, Alice." The Pillar rolls his eyes. "You sound overly American, you know that?" He steps right over Inspector Dormouse, who is still snoring rhythmically, his chest rising and falling and his lips clapping. "So you can tell he's very enthusiastic about the case," the Pillar remarks.

"Dormouse?" I say. "Is he a Wonderlander? *The* Dormouse?"

"Haven't seen him before." The Pillar shakes his shoulders. "His first name is Sherlock. The man is certainly a mystery. The officers outside say he's been chief inspector for ten years. Never solved a case, yet he gets to keep his job—I love Britain. A talented sleeper, I must admit."

"Curiouser and curiouser," I mumble. "I mean, a police officer asleep at the crime scene?"

"There are politicians asleep at their desks, doctors at the operating table, and irresponsible parents drunk at the wheel," the Pillar says, amusing himself. "I'd say this man isn't *that* guilty. There is no real crime scene here, after all. We're just looking for a missing rabbit." The Pillar knocks his cane hard against the floor. "Let's see if the inspector can be of any help."

Inspector Dormouse flips awake, rubbing his beady eyes.

Chapter 4

Sunday, 8:40 a.m.

"So you two are from the animal rights movement?" Inspector Dormouse rubs his eyes. He seems like a decent man to me. Hardly a Wonderland Monster. "My daughter has a hamster, a turtle, and a lizard. She loves animals." He chuckles, rubbing his thick neck. "I hate it when they follow me to the bathroom, but I can't break my daughter's heart."

Pretending we're from the animal rights movement now makes sense to me. Otherwise, we could not have been allowed into the crime scene. As animal enthusiasts, it makes sense to look after the rabbit. Someone should care for the animal, not just humans. Ironically enough, it's the insane who care.

"Amy Watson, my assistant, loves rabbits a lot," the Pillar says—partially making fun of me.

I wonder if we'll be solving crimes with the police from now on. Not a bad idea. We could use some help, as long as they don't know who we really are.

"Amy Watson has been in a rabbit hole once," the Pillar whispers to Inspector Dormouse, then smiles broadly at me.

Unexpectedly, Inspector Dormouse doesn't respond to that. He falls asleep while standing up. His lips ripple like a reluctant wave when he snores.

"Inspector?" I tilt my head, trying to be nice.

"Huh." His eyes flip open again. He rubs them and yawns.

"Apologies. How rude of me. Haven't slept much lately," he says. "Have been working twenty-four-seven since they invented the DOI."

"DOI?" the Pillar says.

"Department of Insanity," Inspector Dormouse says.

"Department of Insanity?" I exchange looks with the Pillar.

"Aye." Inspector Dormouse pulls out a bottle of eye drops and uses it on his eyes. "A few years ago the police noticed a lot of crimes with an unusual insanity factor. Crimes which no one had ever heard of before; like this one, a bunny sent out with a bomb." He chuckles again. His hands shake and he drops the liquid on his cheek. "The world has gone insane."

"I'm glad you noticed." The Pillar squints, but I know what he is thinking. If the police noticed the absurdity of crimes recently, then it probably has to do with the Wonderland Monsters being set loose.

"So you found any leads to the rabbit's whereabouts?" the inspector asks.

"I think we did," the Pillar says, pointing his cane at the sand in the circle, now that he has a much better view from up here. "The Hatter's first clue."

I focus immediately on the ring, trying to figure out the message. Inspector Dormouse yawns, utterly perplexed.

Then I see the clue.

Someone used a stick or something and wrote a message in the sand. The letters are enormous—the Pillar couldn't read them standing too close at the foot of the tiers. Now, we both see it clearly. It's a one-word message:

"Piccadilly?" I say.

"Is this intentional?" Inspector Dormouse scratches his head.

"It is." The Pillar's face looks serious. "This isn't just about a lost rabbit with a bomb. I assume we'll be introduced to a series of clues once we get past this one."

"But there is no clue," Inspector Dormouse counters. "It's just a word. Someone's name, probably."

"You think it's the Hatter's real name?" I cut in, facing the Pillar.

"No," the Pillar says. "The word 'Piccadilly' is written inside a circle. Not the ring, but the one carved with the stick around the word."

I tiptoe and look down to grasp the whole picture. "I see it. A code? Part word and part drawing?"

The Pillar nods.

"Piccadilly Circle?" I interpret. "Is that somewhere we need to go?" Then I get it. "This is where we should look for the rabbit if we want to stop it."

"Yes," the Pillar says. Inspector Dormouse looks at us like two loons from outer space—which we might be. "But it's not Piccadilly Circle. There is no place called Piccadilly Circle. It's Piccadilly Circus, the famous road junction in London."

"How do you know it's 'Circus,' not 'Circle'?" I say.

"Circus is Latin for circle," the Pillar explains. "The so-called Hatter wants to play a game."

"Are you saying the bomb, I mean the rabbit, is in Piccadilly Circus in London?" Inspector Dormouse has awakened again.

"Looks like it," the Pillar says.

"Then we have to go there," I insist. "How much time do we have before the bomb goes off?"

"666 minutes." Inspector Dormouse finally knows something. "That's what the children said the digital timer showed on the bomb."

"That's eleven hours and six minutes." The Pillar looks at his pocket watch. "The rabbit was set loose 12:00 p.m. yesterday, so the bomb should explode 11:06 a.m. today. It's 8:46 a.m. now. We've only got very little time before the bomb goes off!"

Chapter 5

8:49 a.m.

Inspector Dormouse allows us to ride along in the backseat with the police force to Piccadilly Circus. The police force, or rather the Department of Insanity, is frantic, dispatching and calling other institutions.

A bomb about to explode in about an hour and half.

The police make sure the press doesn't know about it. They call 999 and confirm no one is allowed to pass the news of a loose rabbit with a bomb. No need to turn Piccadilly Circus, and London, into a real circus. At least not now.

"But how can he know the rabbit is in Piccadilly Circus?" I ask in the backseat. "I mean, it's a rabbit, not something you control with a remote control."

Although I am expecting insight from Inspector Dormouse, I don't get any. He is already comatose, snoring in the passenger seat. The officer driving smiles feebly at me in the mirror.

"I have no idea," the Pillar replies. "This Hatter wants to play a game. Right now, it's his rules, until we figure out what's on his mind." He pokes Inspector Dormouse with his cane from the back. He still doesn't wake up. "Dedicated sleeper," the Pillar comments, almost admiringly. "Is he always like that?" he asks the driving officer.

"Most of the time." The officer is embarrassed too. "But he is a bloody good inspector."

The Pillar rolls his eyes. "Tell me"—he turns to me—"what happened with Jack?"

"That's none of your business." I don't know why I'm defensive about it. Maybe because I don't want to remember.

However, the Pillar shoots me another admiring look, as if he likes the way I fired back at him.

"So are we there yet?" Inspector Dormouse snaps awake.

"Soon enough, sir," the officer replies.

"Do you dream when you sleep or do you just pass out?" The Pillar is curious.

"Was I asleep?" The inspector scratches his head and yawns.

I smile. The inspector seems to posses the rare capability to shock the Pillar.

"Did I tell you the Hatter told the children about that one girl that could stop the bomb?" Inspector Dormouse says.

"One girl?" I raise an eyebrow.

"Is her name Alice?" The Pillar doesn't waste time.

"No." Inspector Dormouse's beady eyes promise he'll fall asleep again. But before he passes out, he answers us. "Mary Ann, the children said."

"Mary Ann?" I look at the Pillar.

"Who is Mary Ann?" we both utter in one breath.

Chapter 6

Piccadilly Circus, London, 9:06 a.m.

Piccadilly Circus isn't a real circus. It's some sort of a traffic junction, more of a public space at London's West End. It's a busy meeting place. Sometimes, a tourist attraction for those who love noisy and overcrowded places.

"It's been said that a person who stays long enough at Piccadilly Circus would eventually bump into everyone they know." The Pillar sighs as the vehicle stops. The police officer wakes up the inspector, telling him we've arrived. He also tells the inspector to wipe away the words written with a marker on his forehead:

Inspector Sherlock Dormouse

Was miraculously awake from 9:02-9:04.

May he sleep in peace.

"Who did that!" the inspector barks, staring in the rearview mirror.

"It's him." The Pillar points at the officer, when it was him who did it a second ago. "But we're in a hurry. Let's get out, Alice." He takes my hand, and I follow him outside while the inspector punishes the innocent officer in the car.

"Now we're free to begin our investigation alone," the Pillar says, "tell me if you see anything out of the ordinary in the circus."

Piccadilly Circus is full of video displays and neon signs

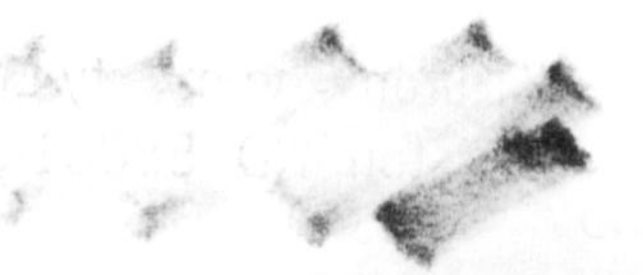

mounted on every building on the northern side. Even this early, it throngs with all kinds of people.

In a hurry, I glimpse a few notable buildings, including the London Pavilion, Criterion Restaurant, and Criterion Theatre. How are we supposed to find a rabbit in this humongous place?

"I don't know what I am looking for," I say.

"You're right. Come with me," the Pillar demands. "There is no way we're going to find clues in all this mess."

"Don't you think Mary Ann is the clue, not Piccadilly Circus?" I ask.

"I don't know who Mary Ann is," he says. "Until we do, this crowded place is all we've got."

I follow the Pillar, glimpsing the time on my watch. It's already 9:07 a.m.

As we snake our way through the crowd and cars, I see a tube station, part of the London Underground system. I wonder if the rabbit ventured down there. I hope not.

"We have to get a better look from the top." The Pillar enters a building and runs up the stairs.

Climbing up, we're trying not to infect others with our panic. So far, no one knows about the bomb that is about to explode in London.

The view from the top is even more confusing. It's like a Caucus Race down there. People walking in every direction. I can't seem to locate most of the police officers.

"This doesn't look good." The Pillar sighs. "It doesn't look like there are clues for us here. And I wouldn't expect to see the rabbit if it's hopping down there."

I concentrate, trying to find the next clue, but it's like looking for a needle in a haystack. I wonder if the Pillar is right about this. Are we really supposed to find the rabbit here? And why hasn't this Hatter contacted us if he wants to play games?

9:09 a.m.

"What's that?" I point at a notable statue in the middle of the circus. It's of a winged, nude man, pointing a bow and string down at the tourists. "Is that Eros?"

"Eros to the Greek, Cupid to the Roman," the Pillar says, still looking lost. "It's one of London's most famous landmarks. But you must know that."

"I know a little about it," I say, although I hardly remember being here before. "Tell me more about it."

"We don't have time, Alice," the Pillar scoffs.

"But what if it's the clue?" I argue. "As far as I see, it's the most eye-catching landmark in this crowded place. It certainly stands out."

"You've got a point." The Pillar stares with interest. "The statue is one of London's icons." He starts reciting facts in case they may lead us somewhere. "It was the first in the world to be cast in aluminum. It's set on a bronze fountain, designed by Alfred Gilbert. It's the symbol of love, but everyone knows that."

"That doesn't sound like something the Hatter wants us to

inspect." I rub my chin, disappointed.

An imaginary bomb is ticking in the back of my head. The sight of a blown-out rabbit drives me crazy. Who would do such a thing?

"Wait," the Pillar says. "The statue is erected upon a fountain, which is called Shaftesbury Memorial Fountain. It commemorates the philanthropic works of Lord Shaftesbury, a famous Victorian politician."

"Victorian?" I say. "You mean he lived in Lewis Carroll's time?"

"True." The Pillar's eyes glitter. "Lord Shaftesbury was also very interested in children, like Lewis. He was one of the first people who argued with Parliament that children shouldn't be working so many hours like they did back then."

"And?" I am excited we might be closing in on the next clue.

"And nothing." The Pillar pouts again. "All similarities stop here. I told you, this statue can't be the clue." He glances at his pocket watch. "It's 9:10. That's so Jub Jub."

"Why send us to such a crowded place?" I look down at the circus, wishing I could see a man with a huge hat and teacups. I remember seeing such a man in the Fat Duck restaurant, where Sir Elton John was playing. "Could the Cheshire be involved in this again?"

"Nah," the Pillar says. "This is... I don't know... different."

"How are we supposed to find more clues here?" I mumble.

"This all seems too out there." Then it strikes me. I hope I'm not too late. "Unless...!"

"Unless what?" He looks defeated, angry he can't solve the puzzle.

"Unless the Hatter has no intentions of letting us stop the bomb," I say. "What if he is like the Muffin Man? Maybe we're here to witness something."

The Pillar cuts me off. "Are you saying we've been led here to die in the bombing?"

Chapter 7

Queen's Garden, Buckingham Palace, London,

9:08 a.m.

"Off with its head!" The Queen of England moaned at her flamingo, the one that was choking in the chubby grip of her hands.

This was the third time she'd ordered a flamingo's head chopped off today, and she was starting to lose her patience.

The Queen was fond of using her flamingos instead of mallets in her favorite game, croquet. She'd flip the flamingo upside down and swing it against the ball with a flat grin on her face.

But in this new world, nothing worked the Queen's way—the Wonderland way.

"What seems to be upsetting you, My Queen?" Margaret Kent, the Duchess, asked, hands politely behind her back while admiring her queen kicking balls.

"Those flamingos are of no use to me." The Queen huffed. "Whenever I swing and am about to hit the ball, the stupid bird flips its head up to avoid the hit. This is nonsense!" She stamped her feet, which made her whole body *boing*, since she was noticeably short.

Margaret Kent took a moment before saying anything. In truth, this wasn't nonsense. Being able to hit a ball with a flamingo's head, like in Wonderland, *that* was nonsense. But how could she persuade someone used to nonsense that what actually made sense was only nonsense to them? Margaret Kent winced at the last thought. It was mind-boggling.

"The flamingos in this world are just animals," Margaret explained. "They will instinctually pull their head back when it's about to hit the ball. It's the normal thing to do."

"Is it normal to disobey the Queen in the this world?" The Queen pouted like a spoiled six-year-old.

"Of course not, My Queen," Margaret said. "It's just that we're not in Wonderland anymore."

"You make it sound like we're aliens who landed on earth."

Margaret didn't comment, but it was a plausible metaphor. Wonderlanders suffered in this world. The real world's nonsense was certainly different from Wonderland's nonsense. Not all nonsense was actually *nonsense.* "Would you like me to order you real mallets instead, My Queen?"

"What's the fun in that?" the Queen said, holding her poor and scared flamingo upside down. "I want you to find a way to convince the flamingo to not flip its head so I can hit the ball with its head."

"Hmm..." Margaret sighed. "I don't know how to do that, My Queen."

"Find a way!" The Queen stamped her feet again. "Bribe it!"

"How?" Margaret was sincere about it. *How do you bribe a flamingo? Give it money? What would it do with it?* No sane flamingo would agree to its own death, even in an insane world.

"Then bring all the toilet paper you can find; wrap it around its neck so it can't flip its head," the Queen shouted.

"Okay?" Margaret squinted hesitantly.

"Or even better, I have another idea."

"Which is?"

"Off with its head!" She waved the flamingo at her guard to take care of the bird.

But the Queen's guards, wearing their bearskin caps and scarlet tunics with the dark blue collars, failed to execute the bird. Whenever they were about to chop its head, the sneaky flamingo pulled it back again, and the guard only sliced thin air.

"What's wrong with this flamingo?" the Queen said. "It doesn't want to hit the ball with its head, and it doesn't want to die."

"It's—" Margaret bowed, wanting to comfort her.

"Shhh." The Queen raised a forefinger in the air. "I'm thinking, Margaret. Don't interrupt my genius thinking."

"But of course, My Queen." In truth, Margaret worried whenever the Queen started *thinking*.

"I finally know what's wrong with this flamingo." The Queen snapped her fingers.

"Enlighten me, please, My Queen."

"It needs a psychiatrist," the Queen whispered, eyes bulging with the revelation.

"A psychiatrist?"

"Yes. Yes." The Queen shook her head, snickering along. "The flamingo is insane. It needs therapy—like every disobeying citizen. Then it will just follow my orders the way I want. Guards!" She turned and clapped the fatty hands. "Send this flamingo to the Radcliffe Lunatic Asylum!"

The Queen's guards did. Immediately.

They took the poor bird, wrapped it in a straitjacket—the Queen had a lot of those scattered all over the palace, but no one really knew why—and then caged the flamingo in the back of an ambulance.

"I hope you're satisfied now." Margaret watched the guards leave the croquet field.

"I'm a queen, Margaret. I'm never satisfied. But I feel better." She inhaled the foggy air with closed eyes.

"Can I talk to you about the Event, now?" Margaret said, as she had wanted to bring it up all day.

"Ah." The Queen waved a hand in the air. "That event! I bet it's going to be marvelous. Have you invited everyone on my list?"

"Yes." Margaret nodded obediently.

"Each and every one of them?"

"From all lands in the world, all ethnicities and tribes," Margaret said. "The crème de la crème of the world's most important people are hours away from arriving."

The Queen smirked, looking at her reflection in the mirror. At first, she was shocked by her image, then she pretended it was the most beautiful in the world. "It's time for the greatest event in the twentieth century to take place."

"It's the twenty-first century, My Queen," Margaret corrected her.

"Who said that?" the Queen said in anger.

Margaret didn't know how to answer that. How could she reason that a fact was, in fact, a fact?

"Doesn't matter." The Queen relaxed again. "Once the Event takes place, and I convince the world with my plan, I can pretty much do what I want with the world, even if I want to change history and time itself—and, of course, every damn flamingo will obey me without a question."

Chapter 8

Top of a building, Piccadilly Circus, London,

9:21 a.m.

"But it can't be that easy," I say, contradicting my previous assumption about us being led here to die. Blame it on my insanity, I guess. "I'm confused about this bomb. I really don't know how to stop it."

"I think you were right." The Pillar snaps his fingers. "Not about being led here to die, but about the statue being the clue."

"How so? Tell me. We have so little time."

"There is something peculiar about the Eros statue," he says. "I remember someone telling me that if it were to release its arrow, its shaft would bury itself in Shaftesbury Avenue down there."

"The statue is pointing at a specific destination?" I squeak. "That must be it. The arrow, within this crowd, is a peculiar landmark. It could be like an X marks the spot. Maybe it leads to the rabbit's whereabouts."

I am already running for the stairs. The Pillar follows me down.

We reach the street below. It's already 9:23 a.m., and I dash through the crowd, toward the statue, tolerating all kinds of vulgar insults for my behavior.

The Pillar stands next to me, our backs to the statue. We follow the arrow's target, and can see it's exactly pointing at something.

A homeless man...

The man is standing fixed in place, as if someone led him to this precise spot. He looks overly dirty, with tattered clothes. The wandering crowds keep away from him. This must be it. The man stands alone, right in the arrow's target. He is even staring at the statue.

The Pillar and I approach the man, not knowing what to say. He doesn't care to lower his eyes at us. He's fixated on the statue, fidgeting his feet, as if to make sure he's standing in the accurate spot.

"Do you know where the rabbit is?" I blurt out, as insane as it sounds.

The man lowers his eyes. His gaze is weird. I suddenly realize he looks frightened.

"Answer me, please." I take a step forward. He says nothing.

"Did the Hatter send you?" the Pillar demands.

The word "Hatter" seems to resonate with the man. Something glitters in his eyes, but he still doesn't talk. He is scared of something.

The Pillar pulls the man by his collar, about to force him to talk. The man resists. His feet cemented in place. Then I see it. Underneath the man's tattered clothes, he is wired with dynamite, and it's probably controlled from afar.

"Look." I point at the dynamite. The Pillar looks around for whoever is doing this. "Stay put," I tell the homeless man. "We'll get help."

I am about to look for Inspector Dormouse when the Pillar squeezes my hand. "I don't think this is the way to solve it. Let's see what this awful-smelling man has to say."

I raise my head and realize that the homeless man has been trying to talk, only he was too scared to raise his voice. The Pillar nears him, trying to listen to the man's shivering lips. The man begins whispering, still stuttering with fear.

"Louder." The Pillar can't make the words out. "You!" he shouts at a few teenagers, listening to their iPods and singing along. The teenagers ignore him, still swinging to the music. The Pillar takes a step forward, pulls their iPods from them, and throws them away. "Walk!" he says, and turns back to the homeless man. The teenagers run away. I haven't seen this serious side of the Pillar before.

The homeless man raises his voice now, intimidated by the Pillar. "Why did the Mock Turtle call its teacher Tortoise?" the homeless man manages to say.

"What?" I grimace.

"*Why did the Mock Turtle call its teacher Tortoise*?" the man repeats, his eyes sincerely pleading for an answer.

"Is this is joke?" I say.

"He's talking about the *Alice in Wonderland* book," the Pillar says. "It's a play on words that we're supposed to solve. It was mentioned in the book."

"What kind of sick game is this?" I lament, then scratch my memory to solve the puzzle. I am supposed to have the *Alice in Wonderland* book memorized in the back of my head, but panic disrupts my thinking.

I look at the Pillar for the solution, and I hate myself for not solving it myself. I want to save this homeless man from exploding any minute now.

"Just give me a minute." The Pillar raises a finger. "I know the solution to this."

"There's no time," the homeless man stutters. "The Hatter told me a girl named Mary Ann might know the answer."

The Pillar and I exchange worried looks. Who the heck is Mary Ann?

"Forget about this Mary Ann," the Pillar tells the man. "We're going to get it solved and save your sorry life."

"Please..." the man says, but then he can't say more.

We're too late. Something splashes against the man's chest. At first, I don't understand what it is. But when the Pillar holds the man tight and helps him fall to the ground, I realize what it is.

The homeless man was shot, probably with a silencer.

Chapter 9

9:36 a.m.

Panicked, I kneel down next to the Pillar, who grits his teeth, pulling his hands away from the corpse. He stands up and stares at the wandering crowd. He flashes fake smiles and persuades them the man has a fainting condition, and that everything is going to be all right once they give him his medicine. The Pillar is worried about the people panicking.

Surprisingly, no one even cares about the homeless guy sprawled in red on the ground.

I refuse to believe the man is dead that soon. There must be a way to save him. I pull my phone out to call an ambulance.

"Stop this," the Pillar says. "I told you, these Wonderland Wars are beyond police and ambulances' help. We don't want them to interfere."

"We were riding along with Inspector Dormouse a few minutes ago. I thought we might work hand in hand to save people's lives by now."

"That was just a trick so we could enter the scene of the crime," the Pillar says. "Why do you even care about a homeless man you don't know?"

"What did you just say?" I snap back. "What's wrong with you? One minute you want us to save lives and then you don't care if a man dies."

"There are bigger stakes at hand." The Pillar looks

frustrated, his eyes looking around for whoever executed that shot. "This sentimental heart of yours will blow everything."

The emergency number picks up, and a woman asks me how she can help. I begin telling her a man is shot at Piccadilly Circus and that we need an ambulance.

"This isn't making any sense," the Pillar says to himself next to me. "Why shoot a man when he is wired with dynamite?"

The Pillar's questioning alerts me after I hang up with the woman, who promised me an ambulance will arrive in a few minutes.

"You're right," I say. "It doesn't make sense."

The Pillar turns and faces me, his eyes looking over my shoulder, wide open. "Unless this is a joke." He points at someone behind me.

I turn around. The homeless man is on his feet, staring at us.

Chapter 10

Radcliffe Lunatic Asylum

Dr. Tom Truckle was gorging on his favorite mock turtle soup when the phone rang.

"Director of the Radcliffe Lunatic Asylum." He leaned back in his chair, trying to sound authoritative as possible.

"The Queen of England sent us a patient," Waltraud said. She sounded terrified.

"The Queen of who?" He dropped his spoon.

"England! Your queen, doctor," Waltraud said. "My queen, too."

"A patient?" He wasn't quite comprehending the conversation. "Send him in immediately!"

"But of course."

"Waltraud! Wait!" Tom stood up. "Send the patient to the VIP ward with the best room possible."

"I thought so."

"And Waltraud, is it a male or a female?"

Waltraud waited for a while. "It's hard to tell, doctor."

"What nonsense is that, Waltraud?"

"I would ask the patient, but I don't think this patient talks."

"It's mute?"

"Mute is someone who once talked—or is supposed to talk."

"You're really not making any sense, Waltraud." Tom sighed, fed up with his employee's stupidity. "What is the patient's problem?"

"It refuses to get its head chopped off," Waltraud said. "The Queen demands the patient to obey her."

Dr. Tom pushed the button on his desk to check on the surveillance cameras. He spotted Waltraud standing in the hall next to a flamingo in a cage.

Previously, he'd always thought it was only the Pillar and Alice who wanted to make fun of him. Now the Queen of England, too?

He swallowed a handful of his pills, without water, and said, "A royal flamingo." He hissed to himself. "Waltraud. Tell the Queen I will take care of the situation myself."

"I will." Waltraud waved at the camera. "And she left you an invitation, too, doctor."

"Invitation? From the Queen herself. What's it about?"

"It says an invitation to 'The Event' on the envelope."

"Bring it to me immediately."

Chapter 11

9:39 a.m.

The blood on the man's chest is nothing but red paint. Was this meant to spook us? I honestly have no idea. All I know is that there is a bomb I need to stop.

"The first time it's only paint, the Hatter told me," the homeless man explains, looking shocked. "The second time the TNT will explode."

"Then why did you fall back?" I say.

"I was just shocked by the impact of the paint ball on my chest," he says.

I look up, trying to locate where the shot came from. I am thinking from the roofs, but I am not sure.

"What do you want from us?" I raise my hands and shout upward. Instead of asking what's wrong, people walk away from me. "Show your face, ugly Wonderlander!"

The Pillar raises an eyebrow, as people stare warily at me. "She's got a Certificate of Insanity," he remarks playfully to the crowd. "She has the right to do that." He swirls his finger around his ear.

"Do you have a problem with that?" I snarl at the passing crowd. I have no idea what's gotten into me, but I am getting sick of all these secret Wonderland games.

"Screaming always feels good." The Pillar acts as if he is my counselor or something. "Breathe in. Breathe out."

"Get your hands off me," I snap. Screaming does feel good. Not just because I've wanted to scream at anyone for a while, but because it helps me remember the solution to the riddle. "I know the answer to your question now." I turn back to the homeless man. "In the book, the Mock Turtle says, '*We called our teacher tortoise because he taught us.*' *Tortoise* sounds like *taught us*. A play on words, like the Pillar said." The Pillar's smile is ten miles wide. "It's in the ninth chapter, called 'The Mock Turtle's Story.'"

"Right answer," the homeless man says. "Thank you."

"Don't mention it," I say, proud of myself. "How come you didn't remember it?" I ask the Pillar.

"Maybe I did." I can't tell whether he is joking or not. "Maybe I'm not fond of homeless people. I think they should get a job." He cocks his head.

"Unbelievable." I shake my head at the Pillar's cruelty. I am definitely not fond of him today.

"So we saved a homeless man from being killed in a silly game," the Pillar says. "How are we going to catch the rabbit?"

Before I contemplate the question, the homeless man answers it: "By answering the second question."

It takes me a moment to realize what I am looking at. The homeless man simply pulls the dynamite off, sneering at me and the Pillar. It's not dynamite. It's a hoax. The homeless man grins, showing his silver tooth, and few other absent ones.

Chapter 12

9:43 a.m.

"I guess you have a job after all." The Pillar grits his teeth. "A brilliant actor."

"Oh, but thank you. I can't believe you two took the bait too easily." The homeless man grins.

"Why would you do that?" I ask him.

"The Hatter pays well," he says. "Which reminds me, he wants you to answer the second question now."

"And why should we answer that?" I say.

"Because of this." He wraps a bracelet around my wrist. I shriek when I look at it. It's made of steel, and I can't pull it off. It's blinking a small red light. "It's another small bomb." The man smirks. "It won't kill you, but it will blow off that cute little arm of yours. Do you happen to know where you got this tattoo, by the way?" He points at the one on my arm. *I can't go back to yesterday, because I was a different person then.*

Angry, I raise my hand to punch the man, but the Pillar stops me. "Don't punch him," the Pillar says through gritted teeth. "The Hatter is playing his cards well."

"Why wouldn't I hit him?" I snap. "I have a Certificate of Insanity."

"If you hit him, you won't know how to rid yourself of the bracelet."

"How do we know it's really a bomb?" I touch it, wanting

to pull it away.

"We don't," the Pillar says. Then he shoots me a sincere look. "But I can't risk that."

"Aw." The creepy man sneers. "I've always loved sentimental moments. Papa and his little girl, the best."

"He's not my papa," I blurt at the man, and shy my eyes away from the Pillar.

The Pillar's face knots. He seems to have changed his mind about hitting the man. "And I don't care if she lives or dies."

I am rather shocked now. I don't know why. Am I expecting him to stand up for me after saying he couldn't risk my death? I suppose he just couldn't, because of whatever reason he has been helping from the beginning. Who are you, Pillar? Sometimes I don't know which side he is on. "Seriously, I've hated homeless people all my life. If you don't tell us how to free her from the bracelet, I will eat you for dinner. Wait. That's not quite impressive. I will kill you, cremate you, and then smoke you and get high on your grave."

The way the Pillar says it forces the man to slightly wince. "Like I said, answer the question." He does his best to not sound intimidated. "'*Who is really described as mad in the* Alice in Wonderland *book?*'"

"The Mad Hatter, of course!" I reply.

"Wrong answer." The man grins again. My bracelet vibrates and blinks faster.

How could that be the wrong answer? What have I done?

Chapter 13

9:49 a.m.

"It's not the Hatter," the Pillar says.

"But—" I try to say something. I am sure it's the Hatter that is called "mad" in the book. Everyone knows he is called the Mad Hatter.

"No," the Pillar says. "The Hatter was never called 'mad' in Lewis Carroll's book. Not once. It's a universal misconception."

"Really?" I retort in disbelief. "Then who was called mad in the book?"

"The March Hare," the Pillar tells me, but he is staring directly at the homeless man. "You have no idea how an original text can be twisted though the years, only because someone misheard or misremembered the original story."

"He's right," the homeless man says.

"March Hares were known to be called mad in Victorian times," the Pillar elaborates. "Probably because they went bonkers in the mating seasons."

While I am shocked by this new fact, I watch the homeless man push a button on some device in his hand. My bracelet stops blinking, and I can pull it off.

Instantly, the Pillar pulls the man by his collar again.

"You don't want to kill me yet." The man waves his hands. "Not before the last questions, do you?" He smiles and shows that silver tooth. "Or you will never find the rabbit and stop the bomb."

The Pillar and I are perplexed at this sick wack. I wonder why people like him aren't institutionalized in the asylum.

The man frees himself from the Pillar. "Are you ready for the last question?"

"The suspense is killing me." The Pillar rolls his eyes.

"Like I said before, the Hatter says only one girl can catch the rabbit," the homeless man says.

"Mary Ann," I interrupt. "Who is Mary Ann?"

The man turns around and runs away. When I am about to chase him, the Pillar grips my hand again. "Let him go, Alice. I know who Mary Ann is now. I should have put it together from the beginning." He sighs then scans his surroundings, as if he is looking for someone.

"What is going on? Who is Mary Ann?" I ask him. "And how is she supposed to lead us to the rabbit's whereabouts?"

"You seriously don't know?" He looks straight into my eyes, as if I should. "I mean, I didn't get it first, but I'm surprised you didn't, too. I thought you knew Lewis Carroll's book by heart."

"There is a Mary Ann in the book?" I say as the memory hits me. It's just a trivial sentence in the White Rabbit chapter, a detail everyone usually overlooks. "I get it now." I feel like I am in a haze. "When the White Rabbit first meets Alice in the book, he mistakes her for someone. The rabbit says, 'Why, Mary Ann, what are you doing out here?'

"Mary Ann is me?" I sound as if I'm asking, but deep inside I know it's a fact. I can't tell why I am sure about it. "This whole game was to tell me it's *me*? Why?"

I am utterly, madly, deeply confused.

"Doesn't matter why now," the Pillar says. "What matters is how you're supposed to have the secrets in you to find the rabbit."

"I am tired of these games." The imaginary haze around me is purple. I feel like I am going to drop to the ground any moment. "What is the point of all that?"

The Pillar holds me before I collapse. "I have no idea. You need to be stronger than this, Alice. It's already 9:52 a.m. A little more than an hour is left. Look inside you, Alice. This is weird, but the solution is buried inside your memory somehow."

A moment of silence imprisons both of us before I speak again. A moment that feels like forever. I realize that there is a big chance I am a nobody. Maybe I was just adopted, left on the doorstep of some church when I was a kid. Maybe I was raised in the jungle among apes and elephants. Maybe I am an alien, and I just don't know it. I am saying this because I truly don't know who I am. This Alice everyone is infatuated with can't be me. I just don't feel it anymore.

My blurry eyes dart toward the tattoo on my arm. What did the homeless man mean when he asked me about it?

"So?" the Pillar says.

"So what?"

"I have no clue to the next step," he says. "You need to help me catch the rabbit."

I have no idea what he is talking about. Not since I left the asylum have I searched within me and found answers. Not for who I am, not for what happened in the bus accident, and certainly not now.

I try to think of my Tiger Lily, of Jack, and of any kind of strength I have inside me. What motivates people to wake themselves up from a haze, I wonder. What motivates people to stay sane in all this insanity, I don't know.

But, surprisingly, a memory hits me like a lightning bolt.

"I think I know the next step," I say reluctantly.

"Excellent!" The Pillar cheers. "What is it?"

"It depends on how fast we can go back to Oxford."

"Oxford?"

"Yes, the house where I was supposedly born and raised."

Chapter 14

Radcliffe Lunatic Asylum

Dr. Tom Truckle stared at the envelope for a while.

An invitation from the Queen of England.

Really?

He pulled out the card from the gold-tinted envelope and read with intent. The Queen was inviting him to what she called the Event.

That's creative, he thought.

The message was brief, demanding a formal tuxedo dress, arrival on time, and the utmost secrecy.

Tom Truckle smiled broadly. The most important event he had ever been invited to was his divorce—even his daughter never invited him to her birthday.

But why him? What did the Queen of England want with him? Did she know who he really was?

Of course not, his mind shushed him.

Then why invite a mere director of an asylum?

He stared at the invitation again, wondering if he should really attend the Event. He scrolled down for his name on the invitation, only to be shocked it wasn't for him.

The doctor gritted his teeth in anger, wondering what this event could be about. The name at the bottom of the invitation provoked him like nothing else. He wondered why the Queen would invite that person, and how they even knew each other.

Something was wrong here. Very wrong.

Chapter 15

Upstairs, Alice Wonder's house, 7 Folly Bridge, Oxford, 10:56 a.m.

Like a mad thief, I am climbing up the water pipe leading to my room in the house I supposedly lived at in the past. The Pillar waits by the corner of the streets to make sure no one sees me. Two-thirds of my climb up, I ask myself who I really am, and what in the world is happening all around me. When I almost slip and fall, I forget all about it and realize that sometimes in life all we can do is keep climbing, even when it doesn't make any sense anymore.

I guess it's some sort of survival mechanism for those who have no clue to what the snicker snack is going on with their lives.

At the top of the pipe, I look down at the Pillar, making sure this is my room I am about to enter. He nods and pulls out binoculars. He begins to track my sisters' movements downstairs while I find the window to my room half open. I have very little time to get this done. About ten minutes.

There is a pot of tiger lilies by the windowsill of my room. It reminds of Jack. But I can't afford remembering what happened to him at the Fat Duck restaurant right now. I avoid the lilies and try not to make a sound while I get inside.

The reason why I am here is the clue left by the Hatter. If I am supposed to be Mary Ann, according to the White Rabbit chapter in *Alice in Wonderland*, then I should also be here fetching gloves and a fan.

In the book, Mary Ann is supposed to be the housemaid, and the White Rabbit says the following to Alice after mistaking her for Mary Ann: "*Run home this moment, and fetch me a pair of gloves and a fan! Quick, now!*"

It might seem far-fetched—insane, to say the least. But I have no other choice but to hang on the thin thread of a clue in hopes of stopping the bomb.

I am back *home*—if it was ever mine.

I am pulling out the drawers and looking under the beds for a pair of gloves and a fan while the Pillar makes sure I won't get caught by my obnoxious sisters downstairs.

Now I only have nine minutes to get this done.

The room means nothing to me. Nothing. I don't remember being here before. I don't remember sleeping in this bed or playing inside these four walls. I don't remember a mother tucking me into bed at night, nor do I remember playing with my sisters.

The room is strangely covered in yellow wallpaper, which also means nothing to me—what child has yellow wallpaper in her room? It reminds me of the asylum. The Pillar told me once that Alice's dress was yellow in the original copy of the book, a gesture of madness.

As I rummage for the gloves and the fan, I wonder if I could sink deeper into my memories. How deep should I dig to get there? Will I ever remember what happened to me when I was seven years old, claiming I fell in a rabbit hole? Why don't I have even one single memory of my younger self?

Eight minutes to go.

I shake the useless thoughts away, and think about saving lives by stopping the bomb.

It takes me a few seconds to actually find what I am looking for. It's too simple to be true.

There is an exquisite fan tucked in the bottom of my lower drawer near the bed. It's a bit old, although intact and unused. When I open it, I see pictures of tiger lilies, pink umbrellas, and golden keys, like the one Lewis gave me. This is definitely the fan I am looking for. It definitely belongs to me. But how is it supposed to help me stop the bomb?

I rummage further through the huge drawer. Far in the back, I find a pair of white gloves. They are small, maybe belonging to a ten- or eleven-year-old. One of the gloves is a bit heavy. There is something inside. I delve into it, and I find a small cell phone.

I push the ON button and look through the contact list. It's the first thing that comes to mind. But there are no contacts. So what's the point of it being in there?

Did I miss something? Finding the gloves in the drawer, and the phone inside, is enough evidence that I am following the clues the way the Hatter planned.

Then I hear a beep. It's a message. No, it's a picture. I tap my feet impatiently, waiting for it to load while I try to keep an alert ear in case one of my sisters decides to enter the room all of a sudden.

While the picture loads, the phone shows a rabbit late for an important date, running around a green garden.

I have only six minutes to go.

The picture finally loads.

When I see it, I clap my hand on my mouth, suppressing a shriek. My stomach churns. I can't believe what I am looking at.

Chapter 16

Downstairs, Alice Wonder's house, 7 Folly Bridge, Oxford, 10:56 a.m.

Down in the open kitchen, Edith Wonder was chopping carrots to make salad. She almost cut herself when her phone rang. But Edith didn't worry. As long as she wore her plastic gloves, it was unlikely she would get hurt. She had always used those gloves when chopping. They helped protect her from cutting herself. Or, at least, they lessened the wounds.

Edith pulled her gloves off and picked up her phone. She read the message. Her face began to twitch. Having seen a lot of mad things in her life, surprising her wasn't easy anymore. But this message was different. Calling it scary was an understatement. It meant that someone knew one of her family's biggest secrets.

Edith put the phone down and watched Lorina breathe on her recently manicured fingernails while watching TV. A reality show about teenagers aspiring to become professional models.

Looking over Lorina's shoulder, Edith sighed. She was staring at an invisible memory. A seven-year-old Alice Wonder standing by the door with a glinting knife in her hand, blood trickling from her dress.

A recurring and haunting memory.

Usually Edith couldn't see Alice's face clearly in this memory. She always wondered why. Maybe because she wanted to suppress that horrible event and leave it behind.

The easiest way to deal with maddening events had always been neglect, as if nothing ever happened.

Edith snapped herself out of it, still remembering how Alice had tried to fool her last time, when she sent that girl from the Drury Lane Theatre to search her room for clues about the bus accident. *Did that girl find anything important?* It was unlikely. Lorina and Edith had cleaned the room of major clues years ago. They had only left Alice's clothes and toys, at the request of their too sentimental mother.

Alice was looking for clues of her past in the wrong direction anyway. But it still bothered Edith—it wasn't exactly the accident that gave away the truth; it was an older memory suppressed under the burden of shock therapy and medications in Alice's mind.

What if Alice found out the truth? Lorina's mind was churning.

Alice Wonder was meant to stay in the asylum, busy with her shock therapies, drugs, and sessions. She wasn't supposed to have enough strength—or time—for detective work. How did she even get out of the asylum? Someone must have been helping her. But who?

And now, there was this message Edith had just received.

"Lorina?" Edith said.

"Hmm?" Lorina was still watching the show while waving a small fan at her fingernails instead of breathing on them.

“I just received a strange message.”

“Delete it,” Lorina said nonchalantly. “Unless they’re messages from cute boys—I delete messages all the time. Mum’s on top of the list.”

“This is different,” Edith said. “You need to pay attention.”

“I am.” Lorina pointed at the TV. “Did this girl really think she could become a model? In a barn, maybe.”

“The message says”—Edith shrugged—“‘*I know about the Event.*’”

Lorina stopped whatever she was doing. Turned around without the slightest hint of worry. Lorina had always been the opposite of her sister. “Just that?” Lorina cocked her head.

“What do you mean ‘just that’?” Edith began chopping carrots again, trying to silence her inner sirens of anxiety. “Very few people know about the circus.”

“It says 'the Event' but not the other word, right?"

"Are we supposed to wait for the other word? Why would someone send *me* such a message?”

“Hmm... Do you recognize the sender’s number?”

“Anonymous.” Edith chopped faster. “Can’t call back. It’s weird.”

“It could be a prank.” Lorina shook her shoulders.

“It seems un”—*chop*—“like”—*chop chop*—“ly.” *Chop chop chop.*

Edith accidentally cut herself. She wasn’t wearing the gloves this time. She dropped the knife but didn’t care to wash her hand. The pain could wait.

"Cut yourself, sis?" Lorina smiled.

Edith neglected her younger sister's sinister curiosity, and began rinsing the bleeding finger under the faucet. When she turned around to look for a handkerchief, she found none. But there was something hung on the wall. Something she could use. A dress. One she had long forgotten about. It was of a small size, and it looked old. Dried bloodstains still stuck to it. Edith didn't want to see that dress. It had been always Lorina's morbid idea to keep it. Edith sighed and used it to dry her hands, then turned and faced Lorina again. "I think someone knows," she told her again.

"Knows what exactly?" Lorina said impatiently.

"Someone knows what really happened to Alice." Edith shrugged.

Chapter 17

Upstairs, Alice Wonder's house, 7 Folly Bridge, Oxford, 11:00 a.m.

The picture is actually a live video of a young girl, wearing an Alice-like dress. The girl is sitting among her friends in what seems like a kindergarten. She is holding a white rabbit in her arms. Other kids surrounding her are playing and patting the cute rabbit.

When the rabbit hiccups, it glows slightly red. However, the children seem to think it's cute. They're infatuated with the rabbit in the absence of teachers.

I grit my teeth at the Hatter's cruelty. How can he do this to the children? It's only five minutes to explosion. My heart sinks into my stomach. I feel this unexplainable haze in my mind, pressuring me again. Should I have taken my medication before leaving the asylum today?

It's only a moment before my phone beeps again. A written message this time. The sender's name: the Hatter.

The kids will explode in about five minutes from now. I can reset the bomb, give you another 24 hours to find the bomb, if you do as I say.

Without even thinking, or consulting the Pillar, I message him back. My hands are trembling as I do. The picture of the kids about to be exploded by a rabbit already haunts me.

Stupidly, my phone slips from my anxious finger. It drops

to the floor and scatters in pieces. Looking at it, I feel my jaw hurting from the tension in my body. I have screwed up.

What have I done?

The clock on the wall says it's 11:02 a.m.

Chapter 18

Downstairs, Alice Wonder's house, 7 Folly Bridge, Oxford, 11:00 a.m.

"No one knows what we've done, Edith." Lorina picked up a mirror and checked her carefully drawn eyebrows, still sitting on the couch. "Boy, I hate my eyebrows. I mean, I *love* my eyebrows, but not enough not to hate them. Ugh."

"How can you be sure that no one knows?" Edith pressed against her wound.

"It's a mad world, sis." Lorina plucked a stray hair away. A smile captured her lips, as if she'd conquered Rome. "Even if someone knows, who'd believe them?"

"I don't know." Edith sighed, frustrated with her sister's carelessness. "But..."

"But what?" Lorina was done with her eyebrows. "Listen, sis. You need to get yourself together. Actually, you need to go out on a date, but we'll talk about that later. Right now, we don't care if anyone knows. Besides, even if someone does, it's not like we're alone in this. A lot of people have got our back. Do you think this mirror is a bit foggy?" She wiped the mirror with the tips of her fingers.

Edith said nothing. She only stared at her younger sister. Outsiders usually considered Lorina the airhead, boyfriend-hungry sister, who'd trip wearing her heals in a party. Little did they know that Lorina was the cruelest creature in the world, even compared to Edith.

“So I shouldn’t worry?” Edith said.

“Damn this mirror.” Lorina plowed it against the wall. She looked like a maniac for a second, but then returned to her Barbie-like look again. She stood up, rubbed her middle finger gently onto her lower lip, and approached Edith. “Sis, you can count on me.” She rested her elbows on the kitchen table, facing Edith. “What we have done in the past stays in the past. We’ve done our part. Others will do theirs. Soon it will all be just fine.” She pulled Edith’s hand up and smoothly wiped the blood away. “Is that *the* knife?”

Edith nodded silently.

“Well, aren’t you sentimental, keeping such evidence at hand.” Lorina rolled her eyes. “Shouldn’t you have destroyed it about twelve years ago?”

“It’s a good knife,” Edith argued. She had no idea why she had kept this knife so long, sharpening it every few months. “You still keep the dress.”

“Ah.” Lorina looked at it. “The housemaid dress. But fair enough. Each of us is keeping a piece of the memory. Blood on the dress. Blood on the knife.” She snickered. “Which reminds me.” Lorina clicked her fingers. “Did you get rid of the girl’s body from last week? The girl from Drury Lane?”

“I did.” Edith snickered, influenced by her sister’s morbidity. Sometimes, Lorina’s ease at doing horrible things was the best way to bond the sisters together.

"Chopped her to pieces?" Lorina raised an eyebrow.

Edith nodded, eyes wide open.

"Good, sis." Lorina patted her. "Sorry I couldn't help with the chopping. I had just manicured my fingernails."

"It's okay." Edith rammed her knife through the carrot again. "I love chopping."

Both girls laughed and forgot about the message.

It was a short-lived moment of happiness, though.

Lorina's face changed all of a sudden. "Did you hear that?" She cocked her head upward. "I think Mother dropped something upstairs."

"Mother isn't in the house, Lorina." Edith's face dimmed again.

Both girls stared at the ceiling until they heard something moving upstairs. They lowered their heads and glared at each other. "A stranger is in the house!"

Chapter 19

Downstairs, Alice Wonder's house, 7 Folly Bridge, Oxford, 11:02 a.m.

I pick up the pieces of the phone and put them together again, cursing my clumsiness and irresponsibility. Thank God the phone wasn't smashed. I just need to put the battery back in and clip it together. As I press the ON button again, my heart is racing. I could be responsible for children dying in some kindergarten somewhere. It seems so random, but even though I know none of these children, I have to save them.

The phone is on, and I message back:

I will do whatever you want, just restart the bomb!

I click send and stare at the clock on the wall. It's almost 11:03 a.m. Did I miss the time? The wait is killing me.

My personal phone buzzes in my pocket. I pull it out. It's the Pillar again. Why would he be calling me while he is watching my sisters downstairs?

The other phone beeps again. It's an MP3 file. I click it open.

Playing the file, I realize I am listening to a conversation between my sisters. Strangely enough, I don't recognize their voices immediately. Only when they start talking about me. What is this? I hear them talking about an "event." A secret event no one's supposed to know about? But that's not the harsh part. I hear them talking about "what happened to me."

What does that mean?

I feel the haze closing in on me again. My mind is spinning. Then the phone beeps one more time. A message from the Hatter:

I will reset the bomb once you pick up the next clue. It's a housemaid's dress, hung in the kitchen downstairs. Good luck with confronting your sisters!

On the other hand, the Pillar keeps buzzing my personal phone. Too many things happen at one. The clock on the wall says it's 11:04 a.m. A surging sting rushes through my body. Hate. Anger. Insanity.

I tuck the gloves and fan in my back pockets of my jeans. I have a feeling I will need them later.

I open the door and dash down the stairs. Since the Hatter can see and record everything around me, I assume he is nearby. But I can't waste time looking for him. I don't even know what he looks like exactly. I do this to save the children—and to confront my sisters.

Chapter 20

Downstairs, Alice Wonder's house, 7 Folly Bridge, Oxford, 11:05 a.m.

At the foot of the stairs, I see Lorina and Edith staring back at me. They're appalled at seeing me. I'm appalled to see them appalled to see me. One happy, appalled family.

Without hesitation, Edith waves a glinting knife in my direction. It's as if she has seen a ghost. The look in her eyes suggests she wouldn't hesitate killing me. How is this possible? Isn't she my sister?

Still stiffened by the heaviness of the moment, I turn and look at Lorina. Maybe my Barbie girl sister will be kinder to me. But she isn't. She looks upon me with pursed lips, as if I am unworthy of her gesture.

Previously I knew my sister rather mocked my insanity and blamed me for killing my classmates. I have been thinking about it for many a night in my cell: what have I done to them that made them hate me this much?

"Look what the cat dragged in." Lorina almost sings the words, as if she is Waltraud making fun of me in the asylum.

"I think we should get rid of her." Edith's face is a bubble of hatred and evil.

"Kill her, you mean?" Lorina asks.

"Chop her like carrots and then kill her." Edith snickers.

I can't believe my ears. I must be insane—*if I had a*

shilling every time the thought crossed my mind. This can't be how the world operates. My sisters can't be so cruel. It must be me who's gone Willy Wonka.

"What have you done to me?" The words escape my mouth ever so slowly. "I heard you talk about me. What is this event you're talking about?"

Then I see the dress hung on the wall behind them. I shouldn't be wasting my time asking about me now. I shouldn't be this selfish. My priority should be to get the dress and stop the bomb. But I can't help it.

"You heard us talk. About the Event? How?" Edith grimaces, and her chubby cheeks bubble out. I watch her face redden. Her anger leaves me paralyzed in my place. It's so imminent I forget I need an answer to my question.

"How are you not in the asylum?" Edith says, as she hurries toward me with the knife, about to stab me.

It takes me a moment to realize that my sister is about to kill me. But it also helps that I don't really remember her. We don't have anything in common. No childhood memories. No secrets shared. Not even fights. In the back of my mind, she doesn't mean anything to me.

I duck, and let Edith swing her knife and slice the thin air atop of me. Then I kick her sideways in the knees. Nonsensical jujitsu style. My fingers tighten together and my hand is straight as a rod.

Edith trips and falls on her face. Her head bangs against the foot of the stairs. She is aching. Cursing me. There is a moment when I want to lend her a hand and apologize, but I don't do it. She tried to stab me. She tried to freakin' stab me.

I close my eyes for a fraction of a second and breathe in. This is the first time my None Fu skills actually work. I read in the book that I should be yelling "yeehaa" or something while fighting. They call it an "anchor call." A word so strong to you that it gives you strength. The only word that strong to me is "Jack." But I can't even begin thinking about him, or I'll start crying. I figure I can do without that word.

With my eyes still closed, I see the book's pages flap before me. Page 82. Line 12. It reads: "*A true None Fu Warrior never take success for granted. If you bring your opponent to the floor, don't expect them not to come back to life. Finish what you started. Long live None Fu!*"

Following the book's instructions, opening my eyes, I kneel down and hit Edith with the back of my elbow, making sure her curses turn to moans then a hissing snore.

I'm Alice's cruel and nonsensical world of madness.

I step on Edith's hand, pull the knife and grip it, then turn to face my other sister. The dizziness strikes again. I don't know why. It's as if my mind is ready to daydream or envision something but it's still too weak to do it. I should have really taken my medication this morning.

I am Alice's sense of blurring realities!

I have to admit it. I feel insane. And I love it.

Lorina stands casually by the table, sucking on a strawberry. My Barbie sister pretends she is cooler than cool. A sinister smile on her heart-shaped lips gives away her real intentions. "None Fu, eh?" she says. "Where did you learn that?"

"You know about None Fu?" I grimace, waving my knife, eyes on the dress behind her. I don't know why, but looking at the dress intensifies my dizziness. I look away, for now.

Lorina lifts her chin and chews on the strawberry. "Know about it?" She stretches her arms and knuckles her slim fingers. "I have a black belt in None Fu, little doll." She suddenly runs across the hall like an acrobat in a circus. She runs backward then somersaults, landing on the couch. She arches her body in some martial arts position, stretching out her hands and calling the fight. "Let's play."

My eyes are so wide open they hurt. I can't believe this is happening.

Knowing the Hatter must be watching me somehow, I dart into the open kitchen and pick up the housemaid's dress. I wrap it around my waist then check the watch. It's exactly 11:06 a.m. I've done it.

My phone beeps instantly. Another message: *Well done. Starting from 12:00 p.m., I will give you 24 more hours to catch the rabbit. That's if your sister doesn't kill you first.*

I look around for some sort of camera or something. How does the Hatter see all of this?

But I have no time.

Lorina is already in my face. She kick-boxes me so hard my back hits the refrigerator. My head buzzes like a tuning fork. I feel like I want to just faint away from all this madness, sliding against the refrigerator door, down to the floor, deep into an ocean of numbness.

"Lorina one, Alice none!" My None Fu sister sets the score.

Chapter 21

Stop!

Freeze this scene. I need to catch my breath while I am sprawled on the kitchen floor.

In a sane world, I'd just let go and call it a day. Seriously, everything so far has been on the tutti frutti side of the world. Why I am fighting my sister right now isn't exactly clear to me. Neither do I know what they meant by "what happened to me." A sane girl would just go away, date a nerdy boy, live in a cute little house, get pregnant, and raise kids later in life.

But a sane girl wouldn't be locked in an asylum. A sane girl wouldn't have a companion called Carter Pillar.

I'm not sane.

Even if I am, I don't think I am—paradox this!

It's hard to explain.

I'm Alice on the dark side of insanity.

And while the conformity of being stranded in an asylum might be a better option, even that isn't working out for me. How many more times can I tolerate shock therapy? How many times can I tolerate waking up finding myself crippled?

Whatever this is I am facing, I have no other choice. My insanity is my sanity. I am both, but I am one. If any of this makes sense.

Okay now, roll on again. Unfreeze that scene.

Lorina sneers at me while I am picking myself up. I have

no idea how she is such a good None Fu fighter. Where did she learn it?

I arch my body, stretching my hands and legs into another position I have been training for in my cell. It looks silly, like in a badly dubbed seventies Asian movie. But it should work out. I stare Lorina in the eyes.

Ding. Round two!

"Do you even know what this position is called?" Lorina makes fun of my average None Fu skills.

"*Zashchishchaiushchikhsya*!" I reply. It's one of the hardest positions—and words—in the book. The term was coined by Lewis Carroll himself when he visited Russia. It turns out Lewis left England but once. Only to go to Russia. He wrote a whole book about his journey and how he fell in love with this particular word, which meant "to be defended" in Russian.

"Can you say *Zashchishchaiushchikhsya* ten times in a row?" Lorina snickers then raises the back of her hand to hit me.

She moves too fast. I lose balance, feeling my cheek go numb from the power of her swing. I plow against the fruit basket on the kitchen table this time. A banana gets stuck in my open mouth, and strawberries shower me as I fall again. White cream trickling on my cheeks. I am a happy cake.

"Lorina two, Alice none!" Lorina rubs something off her dress. It's ridiculous how much she is enjoying this.

"Look." I stand up again. "I don't need this. I came here to get something. I think I should leave now."

I'm Alice's cowardly conscience and subconscious, trying to save the world.

"You're not going anywhere," she exclaims. "Before I put you back in the asylum, where you belong."

"I'm you sister, Lorina," I say. "Why would you want to do this to me? Please."

"You shouldn't have left the asylum." She lashes out her other hand at me.

This time, I've had it.

I don't duck, but face her instead. I crisscross my hand with hers as if they are swords, and then pull the pan from the table and swoosh it across her pretty face.

"If you don't shut up, I will omelet your pretty Barbie face." I don't even know where these words come from.

Lorina glares in disbelief. I have the feeling she needs to check her face in the mirror, but I don't wait that long before I swoosh her face with the pan in the other direction.

"The hell with None Fu," I shout. "Let's do this the stay-at-home mums style." Then I kick her in the knees.

Lorina slumps to the floor, as I feel the anger surface in me. I swing the pan one last time, but my hands freeze midway.

It's not the terrified look on Lorina's face that stops me. It's the fact that she is my sister. Whatever I do to play bad or evil, I seem to soften to the thought of family. The idea of someone being there for me. That I am not alone in this world. I don't want to lose my family, even if I hardly feel for them. Even if they want to get rid of me.

"You're lucky I'm still hoping we can work this out as two sisters." I pant when I say the words. My right hand argues that I should just hit her face and get done with it. I hate my right hand, and oppose it.

"You're right. You're absolutely right." Lorina nods. "We're sisters. We should work this out. I actually like you more than Edith."

Lorina's lie is so sweet I want to believe her. My hunger for belonging to a family urges me to put the pan aside, and I lend her a hand. "I'm glad you think that, too," I say, as she takes it. "Whatever you and Edith have done to me before, don't hesitate to tell me. I promise I will hold no grudges. Let's start all over again. All I want is to know the truth. To know who I am."

Lorina nods, getting to her feet. "I'm so sorry." She begins to trickle tears.

"Don't be." I am about to cry as well, realizing I have no memories of crying on someone's shoulder. "I really need this." I find myself opening my arms wide, longing for Lorina's hug.

But then Lorina's eyes gleam with someone's reflection behind me. I look closer, and I glimpse a silhouette of what looks like Edith about to stab me with her knife again. When I raise my head to Lorina's eyes, I understand how naive I am. She grins at me as Edith stabs me.

I was a fool again.

Chapter 22

Radcliffe Lunatic Asylum

Dr. Truckle stood looking at the miserable flamingo inside the cage, and he has no idea what its condition was in scientific terms.

What was the diagnosis of an independent mind? Was it madness to be different, to want to live, and disobey?

"You're in a lot of trouble. You know that, right?" Dr. Truckle said to the flamingo.

The flamingo said nothing, and hardly acknowledged the doctor's presence, its long neck swirling over its body.

"What's wrong with getting your head bumped into a ball?" Dr. Truckle asked him. "Wouldn't you do that in the name of Britain?"

The flamingo's head dipped lower. It looked ashamed to the doctor.

"Should I assume you're an immigrant?" Dr. Truckle rubbed his chin. "Do you even have papers?"

Surprisingly, the flamingo shook its head.

"So you understand me?" Dr. Truckle approached the cage. "Look, we're both in the mud here, fella," he whispered. "You don't let the Queen bang your small, beautiful head into a ball, I get fired. But if you do, I keep my job. You see, in both cases, no one really cares about you."

The flamingo padded away from the doctor, who suddenly

realized the absurdity of the situation—let alone talking to an animal. "So what am I going to do now?"

Tom stared at the invitation in his hand, and wondered what was going on. A thought occurred to him: what if he managed to use the invitation to sneak into the Event?

He was really curious about it.

He flipped the invitation, only to realize a list of the rest of guests had been written on the back.

Now Tom was really going to lose it.

What?

The names on the list were as shocking as the name in front. Tom was truly losing it, oblivious to what was going on. He glanced at the flamingo again. "Do you know what this Event is about?"

The flamingo nodded.

Chapter 23

Downstairs, Alice Wonder's house, 7 Folly Bridge, Oxford, 11:05 a.m.

Edith doesn't stab me. She screams. She sounds as if she's choking all of a sudden, while Lorina looks appalled again.

I turn around. It's the Pillar, choking Edith with his hookah.

"Such a fantabulous family you have, Alice," he says, pulling the hose tighter around Edith. He doesn't wait for my reaction, as he pulls Edith's knife and hurls it over my shoulder toward Lorina. "No more games, Barbie doll, or I choke your sis to death."

I turn and see Lorina has ducked the knife. She straightens up again. "You?" She frowns.

At first I think she is talking to me. Then I think there is a third party in the room—my mother, maybe? But then I realize it's the Pillar Lorina is talking to.

"You know each other?" I ask, not knowing what to make of it.

But then the Hatter's phone buzzes in my pocket. Another message: *Tick tock. Tick tock. Is it already twelve o'clock? Wait for me to send you the next clue.*

I wait for the rest of message, but nothing comes.

"Let's go, Alice." The Pillar drops the unconscious Edith, holding his phone up. "I'll try to call Inspector Dormouse to arrest your sisters."

"You didn't answer me," I say. "How do you know my sisters?"

But none of them answer me. I see the Pillar staring right into Lorina's eyes. It's that piercing look he is capable of. Lorina stares back in silence. Somewhere between those two lies another greater secret I don't know of.

"I saw them visiting you week after week," the Pillar replies.

I am not convinced. But Lorina doesn't object or comment. She looks scared of the Pillar.

"Let's get out of this circus." The Pillar picks up my umbrella from the floor.

Dazzled, I comply and walk out with him. If I don't, Lorina might try to kill me again—whatever the reason is. I will deal with my sisters later.

"Alice!" Lorina says from behind. "You don't know what you're doing." Her voice is concerned, but not about me. Something else bothers her. "This man you're walking with is using you. Stay away from him."

"Coming from my sister who just tried to kill me?" I say, fighting the tears, and not looking back.

Lorina doesn't comment. And I can't wait to walk out of the house where I was supposedly raised. All I know is that nothing has really changed since the last time I was outside my cell. The world is still mad. Nothing makes sense. And the only thing that keeps me going again is wanting to stop this bomb at all costs.

Chapter 24

George and Danver Ice Cream Cafe, 94 St. Aldates, Oxford, near Alice's Shop and Oxford University

Half an hour later, the Pillar arrives at our table with a tray of food and tea. We're sitting at George and Danver Ice Cream Cafe on the same street that leads to Oxford University, a small walk from the famous Alice's Shop. The sun in the sky is feebly battling through the foggy day. I wish it would make it through, as I am unable to take the dimness of this mind-boggling and emotional day anymore.

"Best carrot ice cream cake in Oxfordshire," the Pillar says, pushing the tray my way. "And also the best tea in England." He sits in his chair and winks at me. I watch him sip with ecstasy from his cup. "Almost as good as the Hatter's tea in Wonderland." He knows that the mention of the Hatter gets on my nerves.

I fiddle with the fork, trying to persuade myself I have an appetite for the deliciously orange cake on the tray. The truth is I hadn't felt like eating or drinking anything since I met my sisters today. They tried to kill me? Seriously? Why was it so important to them I return to the asylum?

The Pillar slides the Hatter's phone back to me. Earlier, I asked him to try and trace the Hatter's number.

"I couldn't locate him," the Pillar explains. "The number is untraceable. Well, not quite untraceable, because it seems like it belongs to a chain of secret phone numbers."

"Secret numbers?"

"The kind only given to people who work closely with the Queen of England in Buckingham Palace."

"So the Queen is playing these games with us?"

"Whoever is playing games is playing with *you,*" he says. "But to answer your question: not a chance." He cuts a huge part of his cake, looking at it the way a five-year-old would. "The Queen doesn't know how to play these kinds of games. Her greatest hobby is to chop off heads. Play croquet, cards, and chess—and win—when she is bored." He swallows the cake, staining his lips with syrup. I watch him closing his eyes and moaning to the brilliance of its taste. When he opens his eyes, he says, "And don't ask me about who the Queen of England really is. We've got a bomb to stop first."

"I won't. But doesn't this mean the Hatter is working for the Queen?" I feel tempted to taste the cake but still can't bring myself to. My mouth is bitter from the taste of my little bloody meeting with my family.

"Not sure, Alice. I'm still working on it. As long as I don't understand the Hatter's motives, there is very little help I can offer."

"Which isn't like you." I eye him closely. Should I bring up the subject of why everyone keeps warning me of him? Or have I become so attached to my little adventures in the world outside the asylum that I won't even risk the fact that the Pillar isn't totally on my side? "I mean, how do you really know my sister?"

"I told you. I saw them visiting you."

"Then why did she warn me of you?" I lean forward. Daring him.

"Everyone's been warning you of me, including Fabiola." The Pillar licks the cake's syrup from his fingers. "And she's supposed to be the word of God or something."

In truth, I can't argue with that. If anyone's the closest to sanity, it's Fabiola. But she hasn't been as helpful as the Pillar so far. Lewis also warned me not to give the golden key to anyone, and the Pillar seems interested in it. It's all confusing and messed up. From another angle, the Pillar saved my life before Edith killed me. He's done that several times before. I decide I'll drop this subject for now.

"So tell me about the Hatter." I need to focus on my job and catch the rabbit.

The Pillar stops in the middle of gorging on the rest of the cake. "This might not be the Hatter, Alice," he says. "I told you that. The Hatter is such a grand, larger-than-life character. I don't understand why he would play a game with a rabbit and a bomb."

"So we actually don't know who we're dealing with?"

The Pillar swallows the rest of his cake, moaning again, unable to answer me. A few children in the area giggle at his behavior. "We don't." He wipes his lips with a napkin, and then pretends to eat it. The children laugh harder, holding on to their parents' hands. "But we're dealing with a crazed maniac, mad enough to kill children with a bomb inside a rabbit. That's *wack à la wack* on my menu of insanity. We can't anger or provoke him. We need to follow his clues and see why he is giving them to you until we find his weak spot."

I let out a sigh, lost in my haze of thoughts.

"Look, Alice. What happened in your house today wasn't your fault."

"Are we talking about my sisters trying to kill me, or me hesitating to kill Lorina?" I am so not happy with myself for being fooled by her.

"Well, Lorina's act was superb. I'm still shocked at how you believed her." He chuckles.

"She is my sister." I stress each syllable, wishing he would understand. "My family. I ran into her arms for the first glimpse of bonding and peace. Don't you have a family, Pillar?"

My question is rhetorical in nature, but it seems to strike a chord in the Pillar. His face freezes. His eyes stare into a distant memory. I wish I knew how to hypnotize him and know all about him.

"I do." He nods. And just before he looks like he'll open up to me, he sticks his fork into my cake and stuffs it into his mouth, silencing his conscience. "You will get better with these emotional hazards once you get your training."

"Training?"

"They say every day in your life is nothing but training for a bigger cause. Like today. You learned a Life's Horrible Truth Number 55."

"Which is?" I grimace.

"Thou shalt not trust anyone," he says. "It's a harsh truth, unbelievable, but with all the madness surrounding us, it's crucial. You shouldn't have fallen for you sister's play." He smiles, as if I should accept this as a fully fleshed reply.

We stare at each other. It's a long moment. I don't grasp the meaning of it. All I am grasping moment after moment is that I am getting lonelier among the crowd. Was that why Alice met so many animals in her book? Because she couldn't trust grownups? Because she was lonely?

"How long before the Hatter sends you the next clue?" The Pillar breaks the tension, finishing *my* cake and drinking my tea.

"About ten minutes," I say. "He said the countdown will start ticking again at twelve o'clock. Ends twenty-four hours later."

"Huh. I'm really curious what he has in mind for you." He tongues his cheeks. "On the outside, this all seems like a time-ticking hunt to stop a bomb. But with all those clues he gave you, there's so much more about this case."

I stare at the housemaid dress, the gloves, and the fan I collected, contemplating the Pillar's words. "It's almost as if I'm in a computer game collecting items for some great reveal."

"That's quite right." He says it as if it didn't cross his mind. "The next clue should confirm your theory."

The Hatter's phone beeps on the table. The Pillar and I share an uncomfortable moment. Then I pick it up and read the message:

I relocated the rabbit with the bomb behind the Snail Mound in Wonderland. You'll find it there.

Chapter 25

The Pillar snatches the phone and reads it. He looks perplexed.

"Are you saying you don't know where this Snail Mound is?" I say.

"I don't," the Pillar says. He isn't comfortable with the fact either. "But you're missing the fact that whatever that Snail Mound is, it's supposed to be in Wonderland. How are you supposed to get to Wonderland?"

"Through the Tom Tower, maybe?" I suggest. "The Einstein Blackboard, traveling back in time?"

"These aren't doorways to Wonderland," the Pillar explains. "These are only temporarily glimpses into it. You can't use them to stay prolonged periods in Wonderland. To find something specific, you need to learn how to really go to Wonderland. Which, in the meantime, is impossible."

"You never told me about that. Why is it impossible?"

"The only way to go to Wonderland is to find six keys, leading to six doors, leading to Wonderland." The Pillar pouts, as if he didn't want to bring this up now. All I can think about is that key Lewis gave me is one of those keys. "Six Impossible Keys. Lewis used to call them Six Impossible Things. But that's way too soon to talk about. This message doesn't make sense. It's another game without much clues."

"Okay," I say. "I will message him and ask him to clarify."

I begin typing my message to him.

Once I begin, the phone beeps:

No need to reply to my messages. I was just sipping my tea.

The message sends shivers to my spine. I raise my head and look up at the surrounding buildings. How is it possible the Hatter sees me?

I stand up and keep looking at the roofs of the buildings. I am looking for a man with a top hat and goggles, like the children described. But I can't see such a man.

I feel like a rocket about to launch, spitting out fire. "What do you want from me?" I scream at the sky, spreading my hands sideways.

"What's wrong, Alice?" the Pillar says.

The walking pedestrians avoid my path, thinking I am insane.

"Show yourself if you dare!" I raise my voice higher, crane my neck higher.

"Beware of what you wish for," the Pillar says sarcastically. "I requested he'd show himself while I was in Phuket, Thailand. Next day a tsunami hit us."

I dismiss the Pillar's annoyance. "How the heck am I supposed to get to the Wonderland?" As I scream, I can feel a slight trembling in my body. It seems to me I am not only mad at this Hatter, but I am still shocked by my previous incident with my sisters.

"You know how to get Wonderland?" a kid who was

watching the Pillar earlier asks me.

"She's insane, kiddo." The Pillar pats him. "Here, pull my finger."

The kid does.

The Pillar farts.

The kid runs away.

All of this happens in the back of my scene while I am panting in anger and frustration.

A phone beeps again. This times it's my personal phone. I pick it up. It's the Hatter's anonymous number. There is no need for him to use his phone again. We're playing with open cards now. He is trying to drive me crazy, and I am trying to see how deep into the rabbit hole I can go.

I read the message:

Find the March Hare. He knows how to get there. And yeah, Wonderland is real—if you're insane enough to get there.

Chapter 26

Queen's Chamber, Buckingham Palace, London

The Queen of England was grooming herself for the Event when Margaret Kent entered the room.

"All the invitations are sent, My Queen," Margaret said. "We're awaiting confirmation."

"Frabjous," the Queen said. "Did you invite the Chinese?"

"Yes."

"The Japanese?"

"Yes."

"The Portuguese?"

"Of course."

"The Lebanese?"

"Them too."

"The Germanese?"

"You mean the Germans, Majesty?" Margaret asked.

"Yes, those." The Queen flipped a finger arrogantly in the air. "How about the Americanese?"

"The Americans, Majesty," Margaret corrected her politely. "Yes. I invited them, too."

"I hate the Americans." The Queen huffed again. "But what the hell. It's all business. We need them."

"We do," Margaret agreed.

"So everyone is about to arrive and see my..." The Queen's eyes widened, and then she snickered again. "Wait!" Her face suddenly knotted. “I hope you made sure we’re not going to run into obstacles and surprises, like the Muffin Man last week.”

“I have taken special care of all that.” Margaret was sure of herself this time. The Event was the utmost important thing on her mind. “I wanted to tell you about something, though.”

“Make it brief—and I hope it’s not about the obnoxious citizens of England asking me to lower taxes.”

“Well, it’s not that, but...” Margaret didn't know how to break the news to her. “There seems to be an unusual incident happening in the last few hours.” She shrugged. “A bomb.”

“A bomb?” The Queen’s eyes bulged. “In the palace?”

“No, My Queen. It’s outside the palace.”

“So what? Put it off?” She combed her hair.

“We can’t. It’s... inside...”

“The palace?” She stopped combing.

“No.” Margaret managed to stay calm.

“Great.” The Queen combed her hair again. “Then put it out.”

“We can’t. It’s inside a rabbit.”

“So what? Shoot the rabbit.” She began putting on her makeup.

“The rabbit is loose on the streets of London, My Queen.”

The Queen rammed everything to the floor and turned to face Margaret with furious anger in her eyes. But it was only for a moment. Her nonchalant attitude returned in a second. “That’s hilarious!” She started clapping her hands. “Who thought of this?

"A man in a circus who was dressed like the Mad Hatter." Margaret was totally surprised by the Queen's reaction, but she wouldn't dare show it.

"Nonsense." The Queen waved her hand. "It can't be him. I know that for a fact. But wait." She laced her hands behind her back and began walking left and right—thinking, probably. Margaret always hated when the Queen began thinking. It never resulted in good deeds. "I have an idea."

"I'm all ears, My Queen."

"Find this madman who stuffed a bomb in a rabbit and send him an invitation to the Event."

"But—"

"No buts," the Queen said. "I could use this kind of madness."

Chapter 27

Department of Insanity, 7.5 Ha Ha Road, London

Time remaining: 23 hours, 49 minutes

Waiting for Inspector Dormouse inside the Department of Insanity's office, I can't help but ask the Pillar about the street name where the department is located: "Ha Ha Road?"

"Would have sounded better if it were Bonkers Road, Fruitcake Alley, or Lala Avenue." The Pillar keeps gesturing at police officers while we talk. He seems to enjoy being among them too much—not bad for a serial killer. "But I checked it on Google Maps. It's a legitimate street name. Maybe that's why they built the Department of Insanity here."

"The sign says Crimes of Insanity, but every one prefers to call it Department of Insanity."

"Well, you can't really call it Crimes of Insanity. If a person is mad it can't be a crime. Thus the diversion, but I like it. Here he comes." He cheers at Inspector Dormouse arriving with his beady eyes.

"Sorry, had to take an afternoon nap," the inspector says, and sits across from us.

"It's not afternoon yet—" I swallow the sentence when the Pillar kicks my foot under the table.

"We need your help, inspector," the Pillar says. "Remember my request on the phone?"

"I do." Inspector Dormouse's belly ripples to his sigh.

"You're looking to meet the so-called March Hare."

"Yes. We have evidence that he is connected to several cases of animal crimes," the Pillar says. "We'd like to interrogate him."

"But the March Hare has been locked up for years," Dormouse says. "He is a very dangerous man."

"We have evidence he organized a crew of animal offenders before he was locked up." The Pillar does all the talking. I barely can grasp how the March Hare is talked about so openly. "It would be a big favor if you helped us meet him. He might lead us to how to stop the rabbit from exploding."

"But no rabbit is going to explode anymore," Inspector Dormouse says. "Can't you see? We're past the deadline of 666 minutes. It was all a hoax by a crazy magician in a cheap circus."

"Again, we have evidence the deadlines has been extended for another twenty-four hours," the Pillar says.

"What evidence?" Inspector Dormouse suddenly seems alert. "Can I see it?"

"It's classified," the Pillar says.

"I'm the police. Nothing is classified to me," Inspector Dormouse says.

"You're the Department of Insanity on 7.5 Ha Ha Street," the Pillar remarks in a slightly mocking manner. "I'm sorry, but you're not really the police."

"You're right." Inspector Dormouse waves his fatty hand in the air. "I hate my job. We haven't solved one case since we were hired a few years ago. How am I supposed to catch a madman and convict him of a crime? A bomb inside a rabbit. Huh."

"I suppose you could help us, then," I offer. "We promise you get the credit if we catch the rabbit."

The Pillar cranes his head with admiration toward me. "She always keeps her promise," he tells Inspector Dormouse, as he flashes a thumb at me. "I assure you, she's not mad like all those criminals you chase. Not in the slightest. She doesn't even own a Certificate of Insanity."

"You look like a fine young woman," Inspector Dormouse says. "My daughter would look up to you. She likes animals and likes saving them." He takes a moment to think it over. His head falls onto his chest as he thinks. He is about to sleep again. "So." Inspector Dormouse comes back from sleep. "What were we saying?"

"The March Hare," I say. "We'd like to meet him." *We have to meet him, and soon.*

"Ah, that."

"Why is he called the March Hare, by the way?" I ask.

"Because he is as mad as a March Hare." Inspector Dormouse chuckles.

"Mad as a March Hare?" I am really confused about this. I thought the saying was "mad as a Hatter," although I know now that the Hatter was never described as "mad" in the book.

"It's an old saying, young girl," Inspector Dormouse says.

"In my days we used to say things like '*you're mad as a March hare*' or '*mad as a bag of snakes.*'"

"Or '*mad as a box of frogs,*'" the Pillar offers.

"See, Professor Petmaster knows." Inspector Dormouse yawns.

"*Mad as a casket in the basket.*" The Pillar can't help it.

"*Mad as the holes in socks.*" Inspector Dormouse stands up and high-fives him.

"*Mad as a parrot with a carrot!*" the Pillar says.

Officers around turn their heads at the two loons I am talking to.

"*Mad as the man in the van.*" Inspector Dormouse looks wide awake now. No coffee needed.

"Can anyone really tell me why he is called the March Hare?" I almost yell in frustration. Seriously, why are all these people not locked away in an asylum?

"Hmm..." Inspector Dormouse adjusts his loose tie and sits back. "Well, young lady, it's because he is usually nervous, unable to relax, always feeling anxious, and everything around him is a conspiracy."

"Did you know that?" I turn and look at the Pillar.

"I heard about him." He cocks his head.

"So does he have a real name?" I ask the inspector.

"Certainly," he says. "His name is Professor Jittery March."

"He is a professor?"

"An exceptional Scottish scientist, indeed," Inspector Dormouse says. "A theorist, architect, and landscapist."

"Wow, all that," I say. "I bet he is nicknamed March Hare for all his talents."

"Not at all," Inspector Dormouse says. "Professor Jittery March is now locked in a high-tech asylum. He is the maddest of the mad."

"Asylum?" I look at the Pillar.

"Top-level high-tech asylum, if I have to repeat myself," Inspector Dormouse says.

"Why?"

Inspector Dormouse takes a long breath and then says, "A few people are allocated to such secure asylums. They say he has gone mad looking for doors to Wonderland."

Chapter 28

Inspector Dormouse's car, somewhere in London

Time remaining: 22 hours, 11 minutes

We're waiting outside the inspector's car, preparing to drive to meet Professor Jittery March. Now unusually alert, Inspector Dormouse is making a lot of phone calls, inside his car, trying to arrange a meeting. I don't know what's really going on, or where the professor is locked up. Neither does the Pillar.

"How come you don't know about Professor Jittery?" I ask him.

"I do know about him," the Pillar whispers so the inspector won't hear us. "It's just we never crossed paths. Back in Wonderland, he was the Hatter's best friend. He owned a house where the craziest tea parties took place. I also don't know what his role is in the upcoming Wonderland Wars."

"You mean he isn't a Wonderland Monster?"

"Jittery?" The Pillar laughs. "I may not have met him much, but I'm sure he isn't one. At least the last time I saw him."

"Which was when?"

"A few years go, in a famous convention where he was showing his genius architectural works," the Pillar says. "Jittery designed most of the world's greatest gardens, some public, some private."

"He did?" I wonder why a talented man like him is locked away.

"You wouldn't believe the beauty of those gardens," the Pillar says. "He was part of a worldwide crew that designed the Royal Botanic Gardens at Kew, for instance. A masterpiece. He was a major landscape consultant in the designing of the Château de Versailles gardens, and the Master of Nets Garden in Suzhou, China. Such a brilliant landscaper."

"I don't know about most of these gardens."

"Just google them. You'll love what you see," the Pillar says. "Jittery is also a scientist. He contributed a lot in studying the Big Bang Theory at CERN in Switzerland. A highly respectable organization in their field."

"Then why is he locked away in some high-tech asylum?"

"This is like asking why you're locked away in the asylum—or the Muffin Man," the Pillar says. "At some point in history it will be scientifically proven that the real asylum is out there, not behind bars in underground facilities. But that's another story for another time. All I know is that Jittery is one of the few who hadn't been locked away by Lewis. He is like Fabiola. Lewis Carroll released them to the real world where they could have a better life. Fabiola used to say she liked Jittery, if I remember correctly. But I am sure she can't help now." The Pillar stops and gazes in Inspector Dormouse's direction. "What really concerns me is this so-called high-tech asylum. I've never heard of it."

"I agree," I say. "I mean, why isn't he just confided to the Radcliffe Lunatic Asylum?"

“I was thinking the same thing.” The Pillar taps his cane once on the floor, eyes twitching at the inspector making his phone calls.

“Do you think we should try calling Dr. Tom Truckle?” I offer. “Maybe he can help?”

“I did.” The Pillar purses his lips. “He hung up once I mentioned Jittery. Tom’s head is buried in illegal practices, bribes, and extortion. He barely tolerates me, so I don’t expose him.”

“That’s reassuring.” I sigh.

“Bear in mind that there is a lot we don’t know about in this world we’re living, dear Alice,” the Pillar says. “There is so much secret politics, moneymaking, and monkey business concerning asylums and insanity. Most of the people in asylums aren't as mad as you think. I said that before, but hey, it wouldn’t hurt to be boring once in a while.”

“Are you talking about me?” I joke.

“Nah, you’re bananas,” he says. “I was talking about me. Contrary to common belief, I am the sanest man in the world.”

Inspector Dormouse summons us to the back of his car. We enter and close the door behind us, ready to listen.

“Look, it’s not easy.” He cranes his neck and talks to us. He has a sleeping mask wrapped around his forehead, the way people wear their sunglasses when they don’t need them. I guess he is planning to take another nap soon. The five o’clock tea nap, maybe? “To get you to meet Professor Jittery, I will risk my career. I don't know a man who'd risk such a thing at my age." He tries to play coy, while he is the sweetest of men. "You promised I get the credit of catching the rabbit if you do. I need to make sure you will stick to your promise. My daughter will be proud of me. She never has been proud of me until this point."

"I swear in the name of the Jabberwock and—"

I cut through the Pillar's sarcasm, and say, "Trust me, Inspector Sherlock. I have no use for the credit. It's the life of a rabbit that's at stake here." Have I just called him by his first name to gain his trust? I think the Pillar's tactics are growing on me.

"Aye, young lady, I believe you. Like I said, you remind me of my daughter."

"So how are we going to meet the famous Jittery?" the Pillar asks.

"You won't, Mister Petmaster," Inspector Dormouse says. "But you, Amy Watson, will."

"But why—"

I cut through the Pillar's disdain again. "I have a good feeling about this. You're Sherlock, and I am Watson, your assistant," I tell Inspector Dormouse.

Way to go, Alice. No wonder you're supposedly majoring in Psychology in Oxford University—where you have not attended one class so far.

Inspector Dormouse chuckles. The car shakes.

"So tell me why Professor Petmaster can't meet the March

Hare," I say.

"Like I said, I'm taking a big risk here," the inspector says. "Jittery is a danger to society. A few men and women are secretly kept where he is. I made a few phone calls and arranged for a meeting. Since I'm one of few men in the police force allowed to meet with dangerous madmen, they agreed. Hesitantly. They only agreed when I told him his niece wishes to see him."

"Me?"

"Yes," Inspector Dormouse says. "I told them *his niece* is my only way to lure him into confessing anything about his madness."

"They believed you?" The Pillar raises a skeptical eyebrow.

"Welcome to the real world," Inspector Dormouse says. "No one cares about anything. Each worker in the system only cares to lift the responsibility off his shoulders. Give them a good reason and promise it's all your fault when something goes wrong, and you're good to go."

"Makes sense to me," I say. "So why aren't we driving to meet Professor Jittery yet?"

"Because I will have to blindfold your eyes and stuff your ears with earplugs," Inspector Dormouse says. "I'm sorry, but no one gets to know the location of the secret asylum. The Hole."

Chapter 29

Flight 321, Beijing airport, China

The man inside the private airplane, ready to take off, was one of the closest to the president of China. An important man indeed, who had served his country for many years.

He leaned back in his seat and stared at the invitation in his hand.

He wasn't quite a fan of the Queen of England, but he had heard about the Event a while ago. It was without question something he would love to be a part of. He and the likes of the Queen had a lot in common.

He was curious.

The Chinese man ordered his pilot to change direction and fly to London immediately. It was about time the world knew about the likes of him and the Queen.

Chapter 30

Secret asylum, the Hole. Somewhere in London?

Time remaining: 20 hours, 34 minutes

"What's a cute girl like you doing in the Hole?" a male voice says.

My eyes are still wrapped with some bandana that prevents me from seeing. I can only rely on my ears and sense of smell to know where I am. But it's been hard to tell in the inspector's car. London is noisy, crowded, and I don't know it well. I only began relying on my senses when I stepped inside what seemed like an elevator.

Now, I can feel my heart rise in my chest as we're chugging down. I can hear the drone of a high-tech machine.

And I don't answer whoever is escorting me down the Hole.

"We rarely have visitors to Professor Jittery." He sounds young. In his twenties, maybe. A nurse of some sorts. "But rarely a beautiful girl like you."

I am getting more and more uncomfortable. Having been hit on twice today is a bit confusing—I remember the lanky officer at the circus this morning. Is that what happens to all girls my age when they're going through their days? Should I giggle and dance, happy that boys don't realize I am insane? Happy that they think I am *beautiful* and *cute*? Or is this the kind of normal obstacle that a girl with a mission has to face all day long? It's as if girls aren't expected to handle big stuff or something.

"Can I pull off my blindfold?" I ask.

"Of course, we're almost there," the boy in the elevator says. "Here. Let me do it for you—"

His hands touch my face. I slap them as hard as I can. It's spontaneous. It's instinctual. It's what I learned in None Fu.

"Ouch!" the boy says. "What was that for?"

I pull off my blindfold, feeling the thump of the elevator stopping under my feet. Slowly my eyes go from blurry to translucent then to normal vision. The boy's face forms in front of me while the elevator doors open.

When I fully regain my vision, I see the boy's hand wounded. I did that? I must be learning to fight faster, although I didn't need to hurt him.

"Sorry. I'm not used to someone touching me, or even getting close. You're cute yourself," I say, not in an attractive way. "Shall we go?" I point at the door.

"You also have beautiful eyes," the boy, who turns out to be in his twenties, with short hair and a muscular figure, says.

"I know." I shrug, playing aloof. "But stay away. Some days I wake up crippled and insane." I don't have time for flirting. Incidents like these make me remember Jack. And I don't want to remember Jack right now. It hurts too much.

The boy laughs. "Beautiful and smart." He ushers me through a corridor of white walls and white tiles. We stop before a white door, and it takes a while before I see him insert a magnetic card into a white slot in the door. The card is as white as everything else.

How do they expect a patient to heal in here? All this white is driving me crazy.

"Take this." The boy hands me what looks like a very small remote control with a single red button on it. "If anything bad happens, if you want to leave, press the button. I will come to you."

I take it. "Don't you have surveillance cameras inside so you'd know if something happens?"

"No," the boy says. "Inspector Dormouse asked for your privacy. Unless..."

"He is right," I say. "I better have no one watch me interrogate him."

"Great. Would you like to go out somewhere after this?"

Wow. Where did that come from?

"I killed my last boyfriend." I am not lying.

"So cute." The boy doesn't give up. "I don't mind if you kill me."

"Listen." I sigh. "You look like a nice guy. Seriously, you don't want to know me. I talk to a flower that spits on me. I have fear of mirrors because of a large rabbit inside it. And again, some days I wake up crippled."

"Wow." He is admiring me more. "You're insane."

"There, you said it."

"I love insane girls."

I sigh. I don't know how to shake him off. "No you don't. Like, for instance, you know Fabiola, the renowned nun in the Vatican?"

"Of course. Lovely lady."

"I watched her kill people inside the Vatican," I say. Strangely, this seems to offend the boy a little. "With a Vorpal Sword. She fights like Jackie Chan and slits throats like a samurai."

"You're funny." The boy takes a step back. His mouth twitching now. "A little bit weird, though."

"Haven't I told you from the start?" I smirk, feeling like I am possessed by the Pillar. "Now, would you like to kiss me?"

The boy frowns. Totally put off by me.

"Nice." I am happy. "Is there anything else I need to know before I enter to meet Professor March?"

"Not at all. In fact, I'm totally convinced you're his niece now."

Chapter 31

Time remaining: 18 hours, 44 minutes

Professor Jittery sits at the steel table in the room. It's bolted to the floor. The first thing I see when I step inside is that his hands are handcuffed to a chain connected to the table.

I step in slowly and look at him. He looks like a human version of a March Hare, if you unleash your imagination. Long grey hair dangling on both sides instead of rabbit ears. A grey beard, untrimmed, like he is about to write the next *Lord of the Rings*. His face is scruffy, and his cheeks are a little bubbly.

I don't know if I am unconsciously comparing his image to the book, or if I'm actually starting to remember things. What really clinch it for me are his big eyes. Bulgy. Curious. Big. They're almost popping out with all the madness in the world.

He is wearing a white straitjacket, but with hands that are untied.

"Do I know you?" he says, hands palm down on the table.

"My name is Alice."

His eyes look like they're about to get watery. A certain sparkle invades them. "I once knew a girl named Alice."

"But it's not me?" I hesitate, still standing, questioning if I am ever going to know if I am the Real Alice.

Professor Jittery watches me for a moment, as if he can't tell. "Well, I was cursed not to recognize her face ever again, but no." He shakes his head. "You're not her. My Alice would have taken me in her arms and kissed my ears." He lowers his head, looking at his chains. He seems sad. "I think she is dead, but I am not sure."

I find it strange he is opening up to me so fast. Maybe it's because he's been locked away here for so long. There is no point in holding anything back. "Sorry to hear that." *Sorry to hear I am dead. Or sorry to hear* she *is dead, and that I am not Alice. Or sorry for anything that doesn't make sense anymore.* "Someone sent me to meet you," I begin.

"Who?"

"A man who claims to be the Hatter."

His left eye twitches. "I don't who that is."

"Whether you do or don't, I really need your help." I want to ask him why he is locked away, but I am not sure how much time I am allowed with him. My priority is to find the rabbit.

"I can't help anyone." He shrugs. "Because I can't help myself."

"That's not what the Hatter—I mean whoever led me here—thinks."

His eyes widen. But he says nothing.

"He stuffed a bomb inside a rabbit and let it loose in the city." I talk slowly so he understands every word. "To find it, he has been sending me clues with a deadline. His last clue was to come and see you."

"Why me?"

"He said you know where to find a place called the Snail

Mound. I should find the rabbit there."

"Do you realize how confused you are?" he says. "One time you say the rabbit is all over the city, and the other time you say it's in this Snail Mound."

"I know it doesn't make sense, but I can't risk not following the clues and waking up tomorrow with children exploded because of that bomb."

"Children?"

"He sent me a video with children playing with the rabbit."

"This man really messes with your mind," he remarks. Coming from a man locked in an underground asylum, I feel like I have to admit my insanity immediately.

"Look, I'm trying to save the kids, so either you know where the Snail Mound is or you don't." I sigh. “I guess the Pillar was right. There is something wrong about this whole thing.”

“Ah, Professor Carter Pillar,” he says. “That’s what it is all about. Please don’t trust that man, young girl. He must be using you for something.”

“So you know him?”

“Of course I do. He knows me, too. That’s a long time ago,” he says. “He killed a lot of people.”

“Tell me more about him.” I approach the table. Sit down across from him. “Why did he kill those people? Why are they saying the *Alice Underground* book drove him insane? Whose side is he on?”

"Let's put it this way, the Pillar is on no one’s side but his own."

"What does that mean?"

"It means you should turn around and leave this place. Make sure you never talk to him again. And forget about anything he's told you," Professor Jittery says firmly. "The Wonderland Wars, if you've heard of them, aren't a game. You'd be lost and lose your mind over it."

"I am already—" I want to tell him that I am insane, but realize we're off topic here. I need to focus on priorities again. "Okay. I will leave. Just tell me how to get to Wonderland. Isn't the Snail Mound a door to Wonderland?"

Professor Jittery laughs broadly. "I wish it was that easy."

"So you do know where Snail Mound is. What do you mean you wish it was easy?"

"No one knows where it is now," he says. "I, of all people, can assure you that. Because I have been searching for it for so long. But for starters, you need to find Six Impossible—"

"Keys," I interrupt. "I know that. Then why did this man who calls himself the Hatter tell me he hid the rabbit in Snail Mound in Wonderland?"

"That's impossible."

"He was specific about it," I say. "Come on, why don't you tell me how I can get to Snail Mound?"

Suddenly, Professor Jittery's eyes dart toward the wall behind me. They're bulging with curiosity again. Wait. That's not curiosity. This is utter nervousness. Fear. He starts to stare up at the ceiling. Fidgeting in his place. "I can't tell you," he whispers. "They're listening."

"Who is?"

"Lower your voice," he insists, his eyes still fixed up. "Come closer."

I lean across the table.

"Whatever you say, and sometimes whatever you think, they know about it." He shudders.

"No one can hear us," I say. "I asked them to stop the surveillance cameras. I assure you, no one is listening."

He chews on his lip and winces. The chains rattling. "You're not listening to me." He sighs. "Come closer."

"I can't come closer," I say. I am on the edge of the table. Reluctantly, I stretch my palms across. I want to gain his trust.

"They don't need cameras to see what's in your head," he whispers. My hands grip the remote tighter. I might need to press the button anytime soon. "They don't need a recorder. They're already inside your head. In mine, too."

"You mean they planted something in your head?" I play along. Conspiracy girl sitting across from a lunatic scientist from Wonderland.

He nods, pupils wider.

"Really?" I am part curious, part acting curious.

"They always do, but most people don't know it," he continues. "Everyone is under surveillance all the time. They know what they're doing. It's how they control the world."

"Who are *they*?"

"You know who they are." He grunts, frustrated by my utter ignorance.

"Of course." I keep playing along. "I just forgot their name."

"They call themselves Black Chess," Professor Jittery announces. His eyes shoot to the roof; he's worried they heard him. I realize he is not staring at the roof—he is trying to look inside his own head. "They're the ones who walk on the black tiles of the Chessboard of Life."

This isn't the first time I've hear this. The Pillar told this to me, and so did Fabiola, but I have no idea what that means.

"So Black Chess..." I begin.

"Lower your voice," he says.

"So Black Chess planted something in your head to read your mind?"

He nods. Getting more fidgety and worried. Now sweating a little. "They want to steal my designs. They want to know what I discovered about this world we live in when I studied science. They want to know if I can expose them. Most of all, they want to know the secrets of my gardens."

I remind myself that the Pillar told me Professor Jittery designed a few of the most famous gardens in the world. Why do I have a feeling I should know more about this? The haze in my head begins to slowly form again.

But before I lunge into another limbo of dizziness, I wake

up to Professor Jittery pounding on the table.

"My gardens. They want to know the secrets to my gardens," he slurs all of a sudden, drooling a little. He wipes his mouth. The chains give him enough slack to reach for his face. "They want to know about..."

Suddenly he stiffens, as if someone has shocked him with an electric prod. His eyes are fixed like arrows at the top of his head.

"They want to know about what?" I demand, infected by his nervousness.

"Can't say," he barely says through his teeth. "It's on. They can see me now. They can hear everything I am saying. It's on!"

"What's on?" I press hard on the sides of the remote, arching my head forward.

"The thing in my head," he says. "It's on. They can see everything now."

"What's that thing in your head? Can you see it? What is it?" I am tense, as much as he is. I think the man's going into a seizure. "What's in your head?"

"A light bulb," he finally says. "They have turned it on. They can see everything."

Chapter 32

Time remaining: 18 hours, 11 minutes

There is hardly anything I can say now, not after Professor Jittery announces he has a light bulb in his head. I mean, I hoped he was at least a little bit sane until that last sentence. But a light bulb? How am I supposed to believe that?

I lean back, waiting for his episode to subside, but it doesn't. His *jittery* moves intensify. He is a tall and strong man. I am worried he can unchain himself, although he doesn't look like he'd hurt me. He is just another Wonderland loon, a product of *Alice in Wonderland*, the weirdest book in history. But aren't we all weird-speaking nutcrackers on the edge of our minds?

"I need to cover my head with something. I need to dim the light bulb." He pulls his head into his outfit, looking like he's wearing a cloak now.

"Did you turn the light bulb off?" I ask, not knowing how to help a man who thinks he's been spied on through a light bulb shimmering in his head.

"I just dimmed it, which is fine." He wipes drool from his mouth. "I buried my secrets in a special part of my brain. When I hide my head under my clothes, they usually can't find their way around for a while. Then they usually give up and leave me alone when they're frustrated."

"You have a special place in your brain where you hide things from others?" I am making conversation until he cools down.

“Come here,” he whispers. “You know there is a left side of the brain and right side, right?”

I nod. Did I learn this in school? If so, what school did I attend?

“The right hemisphere controls the muscles on the left side of the body.” He’s playing professor, and I am his student now. “And vice versa.”

I nod again, a little impatient.

“The left hemisphere is dominant in language, speaking, memory, and in charge of carrying out logic and equations.” I continue listening to him lecturing. Maybe this is getting somewhere. “The right hemisphere is in charge of everything that has to do with arts. It performs some math, but very little. It loves visual imagery.”

“So?”

“The light bulb looks into those two parts of the brain,” he explains. “Do you know in which part I buried my secrets?

“In the right?”

“No.” He smiles broadly. “In the middle.” Now he chuckles like a Mad Hare.

I don’t comment. I push the conversation further. “So we can talk now? They aren’t spying on your brain now, right?”

He nods.

“I need to know how to get to Wonderland.”

Professor Jittery stiffens again. He shakes his head

violently and says, “I wish I knew that one. But you can’t get to Wonderland without the Six Impossible—”

“I know. We just talked about that. Then how do I get to Snail Mound?"

“I will tell you, but I have to warn you,” he says, sounding much quieter and saner than before. “To get there you will have to visit one of my gardens. But bad things happen there.”

“It’s okay,” I say. “All I am looking for is to find the rabbit and find a way to defuse the bomb.”

“You’re not listening to me.” He pounds his hands on the table again. I am really fed up with this roller coaster of emotions. “The garden might lead to a dangerous place. A place that ordinary people shouldn’t know about.”

“Does that place have a name?”

He stiffens more, and neglects my question. “Did you ever hear about the Invisible Plague?”

“No.”

“This place in the garden leads you to the Invisible Plague.” He leans forward.

“So that’s it? Some kind of a plague will consume me if I try to catch the rabbit?”

He says nothing, apparently thinking I am a lost cause.

“Now can you please, please, tell me where this door and garden are?”

“Scotland."

“How is the rabbit supposed to be in Scotland?"

"You asked about Snail Mound, and I am telling you where it is."

"Where in Scotland?" I ask, since I have no other option.

"In a place called the Garden of Cosmic Speculation, one of my designs," he says. "I used to live in a house there, and wanted to use it as a portal to Wonderland."

"Did it ever work?"

"It did." He shrugs. "But..."

"What?"

"It's some kind of weird version of Wonderland."

"What do you mean by weird?"

"I can't really explain it." He seems to be hiding something. "I mean it somehow only showed certain dark memories of Wonderland. It's really hard to explain. It messed with my head."

"Will I find the Snail Mound through these portals?"

"I assume so."

It's not the greatest answer, but I'm taking what I can get. "Is that why you fear the place?" I ask. "Because of some bad memories of Wonderland?"

"Yes. And I wonder why you're being sent there," he says. "I designed endless gardens all around the world, in hopes to cross over to Wonderland. Only this one worked. But it doesn't really work—I know I'm contradicting myself, but I can't explain it any other way. Let's say it's a portal of one of many versions of a possible Wonderland, like a parallel reality. And it messed with my head."

I refrain from saying anything for a moment. Somewhere in the deep end of my mind, I remember having read about parallel worlds, and how scientists assumed there were a million other version of our realities, where we are slightly different people than who we are now.

I think this is the kind of Wonderland the March Hare found. Which I don't really mind, as long as it will lead me to the rabbit—I have faced madder things than a parallel world.

But why did this version of Wonderland scare him so much? And why was I supposed to go there to find the rabbit?

"Tell me, professor," I say. "Why was it so important for you to go back? Why can't you just accept your role in this world as a brilliant landscaper?"

"You don't understand." His bulgy eyes are getting moist. "I miss Wonderland. I am like a child who became a scientist, only to learn that all he really wanted was to never grow up in the first place. I wanted to stay in Wonderland. I wanted to find Alice again."

I don't know why, but it hurts thinking I am not Alice.

"Whoever led you to me, and will lead you to the garden, may not be interested in bombing anyone with this rabbit." He isn't the first to tell me this. It's the Pillar's theory. "I don't know what his motives may be, but it seems a sinister one to me, because this place you're going will show you bad things."

"I understand." I stand up. "Thank you." I say the words,

but can't leave. I feel sympathy for him. Why is he locked in here, really? Is it this Black Chess organization? Are they really trying to find the secrets in his head? If so, who needs those secrets?

Reluctantly, I pace around the table and approach him personally, worried he might freak. But he doesn't. I wrap my arms around him, and can feel the warmth and happiness in his body. "Thank you again." When I raise my head, I see tears in his eyes. Professor Jittery, with all his madness and light bulbs, is the second Wonderlander I've met and actually liked—after Fabiola. He isn't a Wonderland Monster, like the Cheshire. He isn't mysterious with an agenda, like the Pillar.

Professor Jittery is practically a grown-up kiddo hiding behind the fur of a March Hare. All he wants is to go back to Wonderland and leave this mad world behind.

I wave to him one last time and turn to walk out. I press the red bottom to call the guard.

"One last thing," Professor Jittery says. I turn around. "The place in the garden you should be warned of."

"What about it?"

"I can only tell you one thing about it."

"Please tell, Professor Jittery."

"Every time I entered it, it led me to an even scarier place where bad things happened in the past. Stay away from that location, whatever the temptations are."

"Does this place inside the place have a name?"

“They used to call it the circus.”

Chapter 33

The White House, Washington, DC

The man in the room, one of the American president's closest confidants, pulled open the envelope.

He had an idea about what he would find inside, but he needed to make sure.

As he read the invitation, a wide grin slowly formed on his face. Finally, the Queen of England had taken the initiative and called for the Event.

He flipped the envelope over and saw the list of the names invited. He was impressed.

God, if all of those people got together, there would be no stopping the likes of him and the Queen.

He tucked the envelope in, knowing he couldn't make it to London in time. But that was okay. He'd send one of his men, currently in England, to attend the Event on his behalf.

It was about time Black Chess revealed itself to the world.

Chapter 34

Glasgow International Airport

Time remaining: 14 hours, 13 minutes

After a two-hour flight, we land in Glasgow in some private plane arranged by the Pillar.

I can't help but wonder about the Pillar's connections—and fortune—but he dismisses my inquiry whenever I ask. The idea of a super-rich professor favoring being in an asylum over his wealth in the outside world thickens the pile of questions on my part. I know the Pillar will only tell me what he wants to tell me, so it's up to me to figure out the rest of the puzzles.

Once we leave the airport, we're told we'll soon meet up with Inspector Dormouse at the Garden of Cosmic Speculation. It's an hour drive to Dumfries, where it's located. I also learn that the inspector had to coordinate with Scotland Yard to allow us a visit to the garden.

"So you actually knew about Snail Mound?" I ask, sitting in the back of another limousine, driven by the Pillar's chauffeur.

"I knew about the Garden of Cosmic Speculation, but not Snail Mound," the Pillar says, entertaining himself with a hand-held hookah. "The Garden of Cosmic Speculation is incredibly vast, so it needs a specific map. I didn't know there was a place called Snail Mound inside."

"So what is this garden exactly?" I scroll through my phone, staring at the unbelievably amazing pictures of the inside of the garden. Uncannily, it reminds me of Wonderland. I think whoever sees it would think of Alice's books instantly. I wonder why Lewis Carroll movies haven't been shot here.

"There are two versions about the Garden of Cosmic Speculation. One that is told to the public, and one that is the truth. Let me educate you with what is generally told to the public." The Pillar drags from his pipe. Eyes turning beady. He loves it. "The garden is a thirty-acre sculpture garden. It was created by professor, architect, and landscaper Jittery March at his own home, Portrack House, near Dumfries in South West Scotland."

"Okay?" Still looking at the pictures, I am mesmerized by the garden's beauty. It's almost hypnotic looking at it. Part of it is designed to look like the man-sized chessboard in *Alice in Wonderland*, only its square tiles are green and silver.

"Common people will tell you that the garden is inspired by science and mathematics, with sculptures and landscaping on these themes, such as black holes and all that hard-to-comprehend stuff," the Pillar says. "The garden's main motif is green, but it actually has very few and selected plants. People will tell you that Professor Jittery was looking to represent mathematical formulas and scientific phenomena in a setting which elegantly combines natural features and artificial symmetry and curves."

I blink at the complicated words. Am I insane to not understand half of what he just said?

"See? It's all some jibber-jabber, snobbishly complicated talk, mainly meant for you to not understand anything and not question why it looks uncannily like the Wonderland carved in the collective conscious of the world." He coughs. "Scottish tobacco. Horrible." He puts his small hookah away and orders the chauffeur to hand him a Scottish bagpipe. Instead of playing some tune with it, he amazingly starts to drag from it like a regular hookah. "Hmm..." His beady eyes smile. "So where were we?"

"You told me about how the public is supposed to think of the Garden of Cosmic Speculation," I remind him, in case he is wasted by now.

"Ah, that."

"So what is the version the public doesn't know about?" I say, pretending I didn't hear it from the March Hare. I'd like to hear the Pillar's version.

A moment of silence passes before he continues. "This garden was created by the lunatic scientist you met in the secret asylum they call the Hole." The Pillar lowers his voice, as if reading a children's mystery novel in a book club. "Who in reality is the March Hare, another Wonderland character thrown out into this world."

"So what?" I shake my shoulders. "This isn't the first Wonderland character who lives a completely different life in the modern world and excels at it. Like Fabiola."

"Indeed, but the March Hare designed this garden for a

reason," the Pillar says. "The March Hare mapped the Garden of Cosmic Speculation after his faint memory of what Wonderland really looked like. That's what they don't tell you on Wikipedia."

Chapter 35

The Pillar's limousine on its way to the Garden of Cosmic Speculation

Time remaining: 14 hours, 04 minutes

"Why would he do that?" I ask the Pillar, as his chauffeur takes a bump in the road. I am trying to dig more info about the garden and the March Hare, although I already learned most of what I'm hearing now.

"Because he wanted to find a way back to Wonderland," the Pillar explains. "Jittery is one of the most sentimental people/hares. He wasn't in tune with living in this modern world. He didn't like it. He thought it was utterly harsh, insane, and rubbish. Unlike others, he looked for you all the time."

"Me?"

"Yes, you, Alice. He believed you can take him back to Wonderland."

"But you need Six Impossible Keys to go back." I am not even going to discuss the fact characters like the Cheshire did their best to *escape* Wonderland. So why go back?

"Of course you need the keys to go back." The Pillar drags from his bagpipe some more. "Jittery, however, claimed he found a magical way back. Some kind of a cosmic spell."

"By replicating Wonderland in real life?" I am just guessing.

The Pillar nods. "It's some kind of bizarre wishful thinking, if you ask me. I never paid attention to the idea. I believe the March Hare was just nostalgic, unable to live in the mad world we live in now. Replicating Wonderland helped him cope with his own insanity. The March Hare had always been a child in a grown man/rabbit's body."

"So the Garden of Cosmic Speculation is actually a replica of Wonderland?" I think this is insane, but also incredibly fascinating. It means we have some kind of clue of how Wonderland looked like.

"Not exactly," the Pillar says, debunking my speculations. "But it works fine as a map. Meaning the distance and location of places is very similar to Wonderland, although he changed the names of locations to sound modern and scientific."

"That's why you didn't know what Snail Mound is."

The Pillar nods.

"So why does this Hatter hide the rabbit in the garden?" I ask.

"I told you. He's playing games."

"What kind of game requires I collect a glove, a fan, and a housemaid dress, and then visit a replica of Wonderland?"

"It doesn't make sense to me," the Pillar says. "But I wouldn't worry about that now, as I'm sure it will all be explained in the end."

"Then what should I worry about?" Again, I am not sure if I can trust the Pillar with everything he tells me.

"There is something else you don't know about the

garden."

"Which is?"

"The Garden of Cosmic Speculation isn't open to the public. It's a private garden."

"Really? This beauty isn't available for all people to visit?"

"See?" The Pillar breathes out spiral smoke. "Like I told you, Professor Jittery built it to find his way back. There was no point in keeping it open to the public. It's more of a doorway to Wonderland."

"So how are we getting inside?" I ask, but then I realize why Inspector Dormouse is meeting with Scotland Yard right now—probably to get permission to enter it.

"Whatever you're thinking right now, you're right." The Pillar smiles, as if reading my thoughts. "However, the garden opens only one day each year for the public, but it's not anytime soon."

"So why haven't we just asked Professor Jittery for permission to enter?" I say. "Why hasn't he told me about this?"

"Now you're asking the right questions," the Pillar says. "The garden has been confiscated and sold to an elite organization. Why do you think Professor Jittery went mad? And why do you think he is locked in the Hole, which no one knows about?"

"So that's it?" I am starting to understand why Professor Jittery thinks someone is spying in his head. This garden is somehow important in this Wonderland War. Although I don't know how.

“Aren’t you going to ask me about the name of this organization?”

“I don’t need to,” I reply. “It’s Black Chess. The organization Professor Jittery warned me about. The same organization the Muffin Man tried to oppose last week.” I stare directly at the Pillar. “Except no one knows who they really are.”

The car stops, and we arrive at the magnificent Garden of Cosmic Speculation.

Chapter 36

Outside the Garden of Cosmic Speculation, Dumfries, Scotland

Time remaining: 13 hours, 44 minutes

Two men in red cloaks, part of the Reds clan who had once chased the Pillar and Alice in the Vatican, stood atop a green hill overlooking the Garden of Cosmic Speculation. They wore red robes but stood far enough away that no one saw them at the moment. Underneath the robes, their faces weren't visible.

But their voices were audible enough.

One of them, the taller one with a golden number nine sewn to the fabric of the robe, held binoculars. He was watching Alice leave the limousine and meet with Inspector Dormouse.

"Can you see them?" the shorter one, Number 7, asked.

Number 9 nodded. "Inspector Dormouse must have got permission to enter the garden."

"And the girl?"

"She is with the police force," Number 9 said. "It's not the Scottish police, though."

"Must be Inspector Dormouse's team," Number 7 said. "The Department of Insanity."

"Poor Inspector Sherlock. He thinks he is doing a real job. Should we make the phone call now?"

"Nah," Number 7 said. "I'm sure everything will be recorded with the garden's surveillance cameras. Besides, the big moment hasn't arrived yet."

"You keep talking about the *big moment*," Number 9 said. "When is that exactly?"

"The moment when she is closer to circus."

"The circus?" Number 9 chortled. "That would be a *slithy borgrove* and *totally mishmash* moment." He laughed from under his cloak.

Number 7 laughed too. "Oh, man. This girl is in for the surprise of her life."

"I wonder why she is so eager to enter." Number 9 still watched Alice through his binoculars. "Why does she care so much? I mean, it's only a rabbit that will explode, along with a few people. It's not like it doesn't happen every day."

"She is insane," Number 7 said. "Insane people think they can save the day. If she only knew what's in store for her."

Number 9 and Number 7 watched Inspector Dormouse open the main gate to the vacant Garden of Cosmic Speculation. Everyone seemed to hesitate to enter, but not the girl. Alice stepped forward, standing by the threshold.

Chapter 37

The Garden of Cosmic Speculation, Dumfries, Scotland

Time remaining: 13 hours, 30 minutes

I stand before the gate to the garden.

I stiffen. The haze in my head returns. I am a little dizzy again. It's as if I am about to remember something but can't quite cross the threshold of blocked memories.

The garden looks endless from here, with all its bumps and turns. Its grounds, mostly green, seem bright against the cloudy sky above. There is a vast land that looks like a chessboard in the distance, the one I saw in the pictures. A little farther is what looks like a huge DNA helix, made of silver. Farther beyond, I see the sparkling waters of a river.

A sudden feeling of being seven years old again overwhelms me. I want to run the distance. Aimlessly. Irresponsibly. So happy without a specific reason to be. I want to sing all the songs, jump up and down, and declare my existence. I want to be whoever I want to be without even considering the consequences.

I want to own the world again, to be a child all over again.

But the place is the weirdest piece of art I have ever seen, too. It's like an awesome roller coaster where you can't help but wonder if it's going to kill you. Its vastness, as beautiful as it is, scares me, though.

I swallow hard, holding to the gate, as I remember the

March Hare's warning. He told me something was really wrong with this garden, and so has the Pillar. But the March Hare was specific about it: I have to stay away from the circus.

"Do you know what the Snail Mound looks like?" The Pillar stands behind me, sharing my view into the garden.

"It's a spiral green hill, overlooking one of these rivers," I say. "I should not waste time and start looking for it." I turn and face him. "I want my bag with the housemaid dress, the gloves, and the fan."

The pillar hands my backpack over. "Want your umbrella, too?"

"Nah, I'll stick with what that so-called Hatter led me to collect. Let's see what this is all about."

"Great," Inspector Dormouse says. "Let's look for the rabbit with the bomb. My men will spread all over the place."

"I'll be with you as well," the Pillar says.

"I don't mind, but we'll have to spread to find it faster. And I'd prefer to take my route alone."

Why I don't trust the Pillar now, I have no idea. But all the warnings must have some truth to them. I try not to think too much about it.

I remember the so-called Hatter said only Mary Ann can find the rabbit. And I am supposedly Mary Ann.

But why am I Mary Ann? I guess I will find out.

I take a deep breath, as if I am about to take a dip in the ocean of the unknown, and step inside.

Chapter 38

The Garden of Cosmic Speculation, Dumfries, Scotland

Time remaining: 13 hours, 06 minutes

While Inspector Dormouse's men spread through the garden, I take my own route, curious about a few tiger lilies over a hedge. I follow them up and down the hills, as they flare their orange hue onto the place.

But they don't lead me anywhere specific.

Then there are a few other flowers with petals that look like mouths. They remind me of the roses in Lewis Carroll's book, talking to Alice and making fun of her.

I still can see the police flashing their lights in the distance. Deep inside, I don't want to totally lose them. I glimpse the Pillar too. He is sitting over a hill with a bag of carrots.

Still walking, I wish I could glimpse a memory hidden deep in my brain—maybe between the right and left part, like Professor Jittery said. I realize I really like this man.

If parts of this garden are from the real Wonderland then I should remember something, or so I like to believe.

But nothing comes to me. I am just a stranger in a garden I have never been too before. I am a stranger, even to myself.

There are a few thick trees that block the view. A few hedges and turns where someone could easily hide. I begin to hear birds humming all around me. That's when I realize I am too far from the rest.

Looking back, I can't see any of them.

The wind swirls around as the sky above dims. Is it going to rain?

Be brave, Alice. You have a job to do.

But how am I supposed to spot the rabbit in here?

It dawns on me how foolish I am, looking for a rabbit in such a huge place. Really?

Then I hear something hopping next to me.

When I turn to look, the sound disappears.

Then it returns. This time I'm sure it's an animal. I hear it nibbling on something.

Feverishly, I follow the sound, detouring from one tree to another.

Hot. Cold. Then hot again.

Where is it?

I realize I better stay put, so I can locate the sound's source.

When I do, I realize the animal is right next to me, only hiding behind a tree branch.

It's a white rabbit with black, beautiful, and curious eyes. It's nibbling on a carrot, which isn't good, since the Hatter told the children that carrots would expedite the bomb's explosion. I pad toward it, ever so slowly, from behind.

How am I supposed to catch a rabbit if it runs away?

Slowly, I turn back, wishing a police officer were looking my way. They brought those huge nets along. I could use one of them to catch it.

But none of them are nearby.

And it's not a good idea to summon them. My voice will scare the rabbit away.

Slowly, I take my shoes off and pad closer, only to scare myself when I hear the rabbit ticking. It *is* the rabbit we're looking for.

Stupidly, a notion urges me to stretch out my hands and try to catch it.

The rabbit's eyes almost pop upon seeing me. It abandons the carrot and flees.

I run like a maniac after it, memories of the *Alice in Wonderland* book flashing before my eyes. I find it odd that I am chasing a rabbit at the age of nineteen. But I run.

Run, Alice, run!

The rabbit hops in panic. I chase it like a mad girl, my back bent forward, hands stretched out.

"I found it!" I yell, but it seems like no one's hearing me.

Hedge after hedge, one tree trunk after another, I chase what I came for. A rabbit with a bomb.

I fall to my knees, not knowing what I've hit.

I stand up again and look for the rabbit.

Dammit. Where is it?

There it is! Sly and cute little white and curvy thing. With all its innocence, it doesn't have any idea how explosive it is at the moment.

I follow it, but it's still faster.

"I found it, people!"

Finally, someone replies, asking where I am. How am I supposed to know where exactly I am in this endless garden? Can't they tell from my voice?

I must be deeper into the garden. Deeper into Wonderland.

I manage to sprint faster, bigger strides. I am about to catch the rabbit, I think. Here it is. Just right there. I spread my hands. It's only an arm length away. Here...

Then the rabbit suddenly disappears. Like a flash.

How? It's as if an alien force sucked it into space. It all happens so fast.

I try to stand still and think. Not a good idea.

I fall.

The ground underneath me gives in, and I freaking fall.

I am sliding deep down into a hole. A big one. A deep one. I'm falling forever down there. Flapping my hands and legs and looking at the rainy sky through the hole's opening above me.

I can't believe this is happening. It's a long fall. Will I break my neck and die?

On my way down, I see the rabbit flapping its arms and legs in midair next to me. Its ears straight up, a look of surprise in those beautiful eyes.

I realize that I want to save it. Now, why would I care about it, not knowing my own fate?

But I do.

I manage to catch the rabbit while I am falling. I hug it

dearly, trying to assure it everything is going to be all right.

"It's going to be okay." I can't believe I am saying that. "Trust me, it's going to be—"

But it isn't.

My back hits the ground at the bottom of hole. The haze surrounds me again, and this time I remember something. Many things, actually.

The first thing I remember is the March Hare and the Pillar telling me how wrong this chase felt. And they were right. I think whoever that Hatter is, he planned all of this meticulously to get me into the hole. Into the rabbit hole, like Alice did in the book.

What I remember next is more important, because it's an actual memory. It's of Mary Ann. I see her in my mind's eye. She is on the floor, but I can't see her face. Two loony figures surround her, and... they're trying to hurt her.

All memories end abruptly when my backpack drops straight down on my face. It hurts so much, and I think I'm going to fade into oblivion.

Chapter 39

Outside the Garden of Cosmic Speculation, Dumfries, Scotland

Time remaining: 12 hours, 01 minutes

Number 9 was still watching from his binoculars when Alice fell into the rabbit hole. A broad smile animated his face.

"She fell?" Number 7 asked.

"She did." Number 9 nodded. "Deep into the rabbit hole."

"Finally!" Number 7 blew out a sigh. "Should we make the call now?"

"I think so." Number 9 lowered his binoculars and pulled out his cell phone. He dialed the number and said, "The girl is in the hall, closer to the circus. Waiting for further instructions."

Number 7 watched him listen to the person on the other line then hang up. "So?" he asked.

"The Man with the Hat says our job is done. We should be going," Number 9 said. "He'll take it from here."

"Boy, if this girl only knew what she was up to."

Chapter 40

Alice's Dream

I am in the rabbit hole, but my mind isn't there with me.

I am dreaming.

Remembering, maybe?

Jack is sitting opposite me at the table in the Fat Duck restaurant. I just told him he was a figment of his own imagination.

How I hate myself for doing this, now that I see how shocked he is.

"What are you talking about, Alice?" He tries to muster a smile. "No one's a figment of their own imagination."

I hold back the tears. His face goes pale, and I think he's going to throw up. The truth seems to crawl on him slowly, but he is resisting believing it.

"You are, Jack." I hold back the tears. "Trust me, you're the best thing that happened to me in this world, but I can't lie to you any longer."

"Lie to me about what?" He loosens his necktie, hardly breathing.

"I killed you."

"Don't be silly."

"In the bus accident, don't you remember?"

"Am I supposed to remember how I died after I supposedly died?" He lets out a painful chuckle.

"You've got a point," I say. "It's complicated. But your name isn't even Jack. It's Adam J. Dixon."

This seems to throw him off the most. His name makes him realize he shouldn't be here, that he should step over to the other side of this life.

He slumps deeper into his chair, defeated, pale like the dead. "I remember," he murmurs.

"I'm sorry," I say. "I'm really sorry. But if I don't let you go, you will not have a good afterlife. You don't have to stay in this world and be my guardian."

"Why, Alice?" His moist eyes look into mine. "Why did you do it?"

"You mean the killing?"

He nods.

"I don't remember." I can't stop the tears anymore.

"You said I had to die. I seem to remember glimpses of it now," Jack says. "You said all of us on the bus had to die! Why?"

No words escape my throat. I am both crying and ashamed. *I'm Alice's frustration, mutinied by misery, repeated over and over again.*

And the irony is that I don't even know why. "It doesn't matter, Jack. You need to let go."

"I loved you, Alice," he says. "I would have died for you."

I can't comment on this. He already died for me—in a way. *Who gives away a love like that?* I mean, the boy died and died again for me. He loves me unconditionally, if not borderline silly. He almost thinks about nothing but me.

"Let me stay," he begs. "I don't want to go. I still want to make sure you're going to be okay."

"That's not fair, Jack. You can't stay because of me."

"I think I also want to stay to protect you from something." He looks more confused than ever. "I can't remember what it is, though."

"You're dead, Jack. I killed you once, and I have to kill you twice," I say with all the bluntness I can muster. It hurts so deep inside I feel like I'm going to tear apart, blood will spatter out of my veins, and my brains will explode like a watermelon on crack.

"Don't do it, Alice." He reaches for my hand. I pull away. *I hate my hand, and I hate myself.* "This Pillar... he isn't what you..."

I close my eyes, wishing he'd disappear when I open them again. Goodbye, Jack. I hardly remember you, but I know deep inside, somewhere between the layers of my heart and soul, somewhere in the middle of my brain, that I love you more than anything in the world.

But I have to let you go, because you're probably not there in the first place.

Chapter 41

The Garden of Cosmic Speculation, Dumfries, Scotland

Time remaining: 12 hours, 07 minutes

My eyes flip open to a terrible ache in my body. My back is strangely arching upward. I feel like I have landed on a bed with a thick mattress.

I look up, but there is nothing to see. I wonder if the hole has been closed or if it's so far away I can't even glimpse it.

It's all pitch black around me, as if I am buried in a grave.

Where am I?

Well, I know I am underground, but where?

One sentence comes to my mind: *Alice's Adventures Underground.*

When I try to move, my body aches harder, but it's not that bad. I don't think I broke any bones.

The place smells of dirt, and the rabbit I was chasing is absent. I should at least hear its voice if it is still here. Could something have happened to it? I remember holding it in my arms before I fell. If I am not hurt then the rabbit should be safe, too.

I cough a couple of times before I reach for my phone. I get it and use its screen as a flashlight.

I point it upward, but I still can't see the opening of the hole. Down here, there is only dirt on both sides. I'm in what looks like a round room made of brick, maybe at the bottom of a tower. And it doesn't look like there is a way out, unless the light from my phone isn't reaching far enough.

I stand up and point the light at where I fell. It is a bed, like I thought, with one hell of a thick mattress.

I yell for help a couple of times but I get no reply.

Then it occurs to me to check the time on my phone. It's almost midnight. Have I been unconscious for more than two hours? Why haven't the police picked me up yet? It shouldn't have been hard to find the hole. It's one big hole.

My phone rings.

It throws me off for a second. Then I realize it's the Pillar. I realize I have twenty-three missed calls from him. I pick it up.

"Where are you, Alice?" He sounds concerned.

"I'm underground."

"What does that mean? We're looking for you all over the garden."

"I found the rabbit, but then followed it and fell into a hole."

"A hole?" The Pillar sounds skeptical. "You mean a rabbit hole?"

"You could call it that," I say. "I am surprised you didn't come across it."

"This can't be," he says. "We've been looking for you so long. The police scanned every inch of the garden. They didn't find you. No holes, either."

I point the phone's light upward again, still unable to see

the opening of the rabbit hole.

"I have no idea what's going on," I say. "Wait. Let me use the GPS."

"Good idea."

I fiddle with my phone and I turn the GPS on, and try to locate my place. At first, I think there is something wrong with it. Everything showing on the map is like nothing I have seen before. There are no streets. No names. Nothing that makes sense.

"What's taking you so long?" the Pillar urges me.

"You will not believe this," I say, still looking at the GPS on my phone. "My GPS doesn't show street addresses and coordinates."

"I don't understand. What does it show?"

"A map." I want to scratch my head.

"A map? Of course it shows a map. Now send me your coordinates or just activate your location, because I am not getting any useful info from your phone."

"Pillar," I say firmly, "you don't understand. It's a map of Wonderland."

Chapter 42

Time remaining: 12 hours, 05 minutes

"Alice, that can't be."

"That's what it says." I try to zoom out, but it's impossible. I can't even log in to other applications on the internet, just look at this GPS and talk to the Pillar. "It says my location is the rabbit hole."

The Pillar stays silent on the phone. He is as shocked as I am.

In truth, I'm not as shocked as I am fascinated by the idea: I have a GPS map of Wonderland?

"So the March Hare was right." I try to make sense of it. "The Garden of Cosmic Speculation is a magical doorway to Wonderland."

"I don't know what to say to that," the Pillar says. "Why can't we find you, then?"

"Maybe the rabbit hole is a *hole* into another dimension," I suggest. "More of a black hole, maybe."

"So the so-called Hatter planned all this to get you to find a secret doorway to Wonderland?"

I think it over. It could be.

"Maybe all he needed was to get to that door," the Pillar says. "He fabricated all those clues to lead you to the March Hare, who would eventually send you to Wonderland. If you hadn't met the March Hare, we wouldn't have been granted entry by Interpol themselves."

"Are you saying he couldn't have entered the garden by himself?"

"It's under surveillance and maximum security," the Pillar says.

"Then how did he get the rabbit in?"

"Maybe he got it inside after we opened the gates," the Pillar says. "Maybe he is among us now."

The idea makes me frantically circle the hole. Could the so-called Hatter be in here with me? But what are the dress, fan, and gloves for? Why would he send me in here, anyway?

"Who else will discover the rabbit hole but you, Alice?" the Pillar says. "I don't know how this works, but it seems right to me."

"It doesn't click for me, Pillar." I touch the walls, looking for a door out. If this is a replication of the rabbit hole in the books, then I should find a door out.

"Hang in there, Alice. I will talk to Inspector Dormouse. We have to find you."

"Please do." I squint at the walls, listening to the Pillar hang up.

It occurs to me that the door is maybe too small or too big, like in the books, so I kneel down and feel the walls.

And there it is: a small door at the bottom of the wall.

Chapter 43

Time remaining: 12 hours, 01 minutes

The door is made of steel. It's unbreakable.

It has a small keyhole but no key. When I try to look through it, I only see darkness on the other side.

My mind can't come up with what to do next. There has to be a key, or a clue, but I can't find any. I stare back at the map of Wonderland. Knowing there are so many places I can get to right now drives me crazy.

I kneel down and look for a key in the dirt. There must be one. But I still don't find any.

However, I come upon a surprise: a tiny bottle with pink liquid inside.

I lift it up beneath the phone's light, and I don't have to guess what's written on the bottle's label. It fits with the book, as if I am living the Alice story all over again—or reliving it, pick your insanity and go with it.

The writing on the label says: Drink Me.

I am totally aware of this being the Hatter's game, and I know the consequences may be dire, but I have to play anyway. Not sure why, though. Am I doing this to find the rabbit, or...?

I pull the cork and stare at the liquid. What will this drink really do to me? It won't shrink me, will it? That would be so unlike the real world. Of course, I have seen madder things in this world, but I feel that shrinking in size is just too clichéd.

But I suppose this is my only way out of this hole. I take a deep breath and gulp it in one shot.

My eyes blur and my head feels like it's going to explode. The impact is too strong and I fall to my knees.

The phone rings next to me, and I can barely see the Pillar's name flash on its screen. My hands feel numb, but I try my best to reach for it.

When I succeed, and hear the Pillar's voice, I realize I can't speak. My tongue is numb. I am trying my best not to swallow it and die.

Chapter 44

Queen's Chamber, Buckingham Palace, London

Margaret Kent watched the Queen get ready.

It had taken her about an hour to fit into her dress, enough time to chop a couple of heads off in between—she was upset with her servant's sluggish work, so a dead head lay next to her on the palace's floor.

"I'm ready, Margaret," she wailed, powdering her face. "Are all my guests here?"

"All of them arrived, My Queen," Margaret said. "They're waiting in the meeting room."

"So none of them rejected the invitation?" The Queen looked impressed.

"Each and every one of the them from all over the world is in the meeting room." Margaret hesitated. "Except one, of course."

"I know who that guest is." The Queen pouted. "I expected the rejection."

Margaret was curious. "I'm surprised you invited that guest in particular to the Event."

"Some invitations are meant to be declined." The Queen grinned. "But you wouldn't understand it, Duchess. Some of my actions are too smart for the likes of you."

"But of course." Margaret swallowed her humiliation. After all, it was the Queen who was dumb like a drum. But she couldn’t tell her that and risk her head being chopped off. “How would I ever match your genius, My Queen. Should I announce your arrival to the guests?”

“Not before you kiss my hand.” The Queen sneered.

Margaret bowed and kissed the Queen’s hand. It wasn’t an easy task, as every part of it was wrapped in jewelry.

“That’s better, or I’d have sent you to the asylum, along with the flamingo,” the Queen said, chin up. “Now, go tell the guests I’m on my way, and once I arrive I will show them something they have never seen the likes of before.”

Margaret obeyed the Queen and left.

***

Once she was alone, the Queen pushed a button next to her bed and the secret door parted in the wall. She stepped through into what looked like a wall closet.

On its floor, there was a coffin.

The Queen pushed the lid open and stared at the woman inside. “I wonder what I should really do with your body,” the Queen said. “Should I burn it, or will I actually need to wake you up someday?”

It only took her a moment to pull the coffin to a close again. Before she did, she took one last look at the real Queen of England inside, the one she had managed to change her features to match.

The Queen of Hearts of Wonderland wasn't happy with looking like the real Queen of England. That Queen looked too peaceful, too smiley. Where was the grit? Where was the power?

But it was a necessary evil to her—she'd made the transformation through a nonsensical Lewis Carroll potion—at least until she persuaded her visitors with her world-changing plan.

Chapter 45

The rabbit hole, the Garden of Cosmic Speculation

Time remaining: 12 hours, 01 minutes

I wake up to a continuous beeping on my phone.

Eyes still blurry, I reach for it blindly until I clasp it by accident from the floor. When I bring it to my face, I am shocked by its size. It looks as big as a plasma TV.

How so, when I am gripping it in the palm of my hand?

The pain in the back of my head attacks me, and I remember that I am under the influence of the pink drink in the bottle.

Did it really shrink me, now that I think I am smaller than my own phone?

But I'm gripping it. What kind of mind-bend is that?

Through my hazy vision, I realize that almost everything around is much bigger than me. Or I am much smaller than them.

Even the small door at the foot of the wall.

Then again, when I reach for it, I can touch it as if it's small, not big.

The phone keeps beeping.

I push the overly big answer button—the one that is also small—and find more than a hundred messages from an anonymous number.

It must be the Hatter.

What you're experiencing now is no hallucination—

although it is in a way. It's a medical condition, induced by the pink drink. It's called the Alice Syndrome.

What?

Furious, I message back:

Why don't you just talk to me face to face, instead of hiding behind the alphabet of your messages!

The reply arrives instantly:

I don't think that will be useful, since you can't talk at the moment.

Suddenly, I remember my numb tongue. I try to say my name but can't. My tongue is just dangling like an earring from my mouth. I suppose it was also induced by the drink, but it feels horrible.

What do you want from me? I message back.

A reply arrives:

To continue playing the game until it has to stop.

I don't even know what that means. He continues writing:

You will crawl through the small door and find yourself in a vast tunnel system underground. Then, with the GPS coordinates, I want you to find a place for me.

I write back:

How can I even get past the door?

He writes back:

Don't worry, I will tell you how. You haven't asked me about the place I want you to find. I'm starting to think you're not taking this seriously. If you don't, I will set the rabbit loose on the streets of London.

I have no idea how he'd send the rabbit back to London, or where the rabbit is right now. All I know is that I am dealing with craziest maniac I've met so far. I don't think I can ask him where I really am.

Where is that place?

He responds immediately:

If I knew I'd have found it myself. Only you can find it. It's either in Wonderland or the real world. I am not sure, but I know it can be accessed behind that small door—and don't ask why.

My tongue still feels numb. I write to him:

I will do as you say, but you will show me the rabbit's place in return when I finish your mission. Again, does the place have a name?

He takes a bit longer again:

It's called the circus.

A lot of memories flood into the swimming pool of my brain. It's as if I know this place, but I can't really tell. I remember the March Hare telling me about the circus in the Garden of Cosmic Speculation, and how dangerous it is. Why did he warn me about a circus? Isn't it supposed to be a fun place? Unless you meet the clown, of course.

I type back:

If you don't know where the circus is, how am I supposed to find it?

A response arrives:

Once you pass that door, memories of your past should come back to you. That's when you will know where the circus is.

I type:

Are you saying you're one of those who believe I am the Real Alice?

The reply:

You better be, or a lot of people will die. Now get past that door.

Furious again, I write:

How?

He responds:

What do you mean how? I suppose you think you need a key. Not all doors open with keys. Some you only have to knock, and they will let you in.

Chapter 46

Beyond the door, the Garden of Cosmic Speculation

Time remaining: 11 hours, 30 minutes

Once I knock, the doorknob turns and the door opens, and a gust of wind plows against my chest. It smells of mushrooms.

With a numb tongue and misleading vision, I realize I am not underground anymore. Instead, I'm looking at the colorful world of Wonderland.

It seems hard to grasp its vastness at first—harder to believe this is really happening.

But I step forward into a green road with yellow bananas for trees, bending on both sides. The banana trees have their sides peeled. A few birds twitter on top on the edges.

The sky is the color of marmalade, which is gross at first sight, but within the context of all the green and yellow, orange shines through. It all looks like a child's drawing.

There isn't enough time to take in the surroundings. I prefer to figure out how I'm supposed to find the circus—which isn't showing on my Wonderland map.

I walk ahead, looking for someone to meet, but the place seems abandoned.

Where did everyone in Wonderland go?

A banana tree bends too close, as if spying on me.

"What do you want?" I want to say, but nothing comes out. My tongue feels like cotton.

I am not even sure the banana—or the tree—is as large as I think.

When I stare at my feet, they are bigger than the hole I fell through earlier. They flap loudly, as if I'm a seal.

My toe is also scaring me. It's really awful and big. Red, as if bruised. It's one big tomato.

I look away.

Where is everyone?

I take another look at my phone. I see a few locations on the map. The Queen of Hearts' palace, the Muffin Man's house, and big chessboard land.

I also spot Lewis Carroll's studio, which looks like it's on the edge of Wonderland. It makes sense now that I saw him enter Wonderland from a door in Oxford University when I met him through the Tom Tower a couple of weeks ago.

But if Oxford University is tangent to Wonderland, how am I in Scotland right now? Or am I?

It's mind-boggling. Messed up. Dizzying.

I decide to accept things the way they are, just like the Pillar said.

I hate how the Pillar is always right. Trying to apply logic, or even a fragment of logic, in the insane world I am in is useless.

So I go with the flow.

I have a circus to find.

Strange enough, the map doesn't show a circus in

Wonderland, and I don't remember a circus in Lewis Carroll's book.

I have no idea where to find this circus, or why it's so important—the March Hare warned me of it, and the Hatter desires it. The Pillar doesn't know much about it.

"Psst," I hear a female voice call me. "You can't keep walking like that in here."

I stop in my tracks, but don't see anyone around me.

All but a tiger lily bending over toward me, a little too large, of course.

I shake my head, longing for an explanation, as I can't talk.

"You look like you're from another world, walking in those jeans and boots," Tiger Lily says, and suddenly I realize it's *my* Tiger Lily. "You should put on the maid's dress."

How does she know about the maid's dress in my bag?

"Hurry!" it insists, as it always does in the real world.

I take a moment to think about it. Whenever she talks to me, I am usually in my hallucinating mode. So what does that mean now? Or is it part of my induced Alice Syndrome?

Tiger Lily grins. I think she knows what I am thinking about. "Ah." She twists her petals. "You think you're mad because I'm talking to you."

I nod.

"I don't blame you, because frankly: *how come a flower talks?*" She snickers. "But the thing is, who will you be talking to if *I* don't talk to you? In other words, would you prefer loneliness over madness?"

Well, that's the Tiger Lily I know. I wonder why I am so attached to it. Whatever happened in the past between me and her?

But if I am going to comply with her logic, I need her to do something for me first. I point at my dangling tongue.

"Are you bargaining now?" She takes a minute to think it over. "I like it when you don't give up easily. Why not." She spits blueberries at my tongue.

They break open and tickle me, then sting, but finally I am able to speak again. "How do I get to the circus?" I ask immediately.

"Ah, the circus," she says. "You don't want to go there, Alice. You don't want to go there."

Chapter 47

Wonderland

Time remaining: 10 hours, 38 minutes

"Don't give me advice," I retort. "I know what I am doing. I need to find the circus for this Hatter so he'll show me where to find the rabbit. I think I have around ten hours left before a bomb goes off."

"Boom!" Tiger Lilly snickers again. I hate her when she goes nuts like that. "Well, first you need to put on the dress, like I told you."

Since I don't want to look like an intruder in this world, I put it on. It's a bit too small for me, but I force myself to fit. "Should I wear the gloves and the fan too?"

"Nah," she says. "Their time hasn't come yet."

"So you know what all of this is about," I say.

"I do." She nods. "So do you."

"What do you mean? I have no idea what's going on."

"Oh, you do. You just don't remember it yet."

"Then why don't you remind me?" I sigh.

"What's the fun in that, Alice?" she says. "One is never told the truth. One has to find it out."

"Whatever that means." I tighten the laces of the dress and take off my shoes.

"But I can tell you that the glove and fan in your pockets are useless. All you need is the dress."

"They can't be. I found them, according to the Hatter's clues."

"Not those," she says. "You got the wrong ones. The real ones are with the *wonders.*"

"Wonders?" I blink. "What does that mean?"

"It's a puzzle you have to solve, but way later, not now," she says. "*Now*, let me tell you about what you're looking for in here."

"The circus," I say. "Where is everyone, by the way?"

"Everyone is in the circus."

"Okay?" I tilt my head. "So it wouldn't be hard to find it, right?"

"It's tricky, Alice," she says. "Very tricky. I mean, doesn't it strike you as strange that every single Wonderlander is in the circus right now?"

I look around and shrug. It's extremely unsettling that Wonderland is vacant like this. She is right.

"That's why you should think twice about the circus."

"I told I'm not going to rethink it," I say. "Tell me how to get to the circus."

"I'm sorry, Alice," it says. "I want to protect you from the circus, so I will not lead you to it."

"You know what? I'll find it myself." I turn around and walk ahead.

Something inside me isn't right. I know it.

Since I put on the dress I've felt changed. I also feel a bit stubborn and childish in the way I am acting.

It's that haze that surrounds my mind. Those distant memories that seem to crawl toward me, so slowly.

I wonder if I am suppressing certain memories and don't really want to remember. *Why, Alice? What happened to you in the past?*

When I turn back to look at Tiger Lily, she is sleeping, as if she hadn't been talking to me.

I decide I'll message the Hatter back:

I can't find the circus. You must have a clue how I should find it.

He responds:

I wouldn't have needed your help if I did.

I write:

What's so important in the circus?

He responds:

You will know when you get there. It concerns you as it concerns me. You have less than 10 hours, and the circus might be closing soon. I need you to find it while it's full of people, or otherwise it will mean nothing to me. I'd hurry if I were you.

Chapter 48

Wonderland

Time remaining: 9 hours, 54 minutes

It occurs to me to call the Pillar, but I get no signal to the real world. However this works in Wonderland, I have no idea. I realize I'm as confused as the March Hare when he told me about the doorways.

And, of course, it occurs to me that I'm just in my own escapist La La land of my mind, evading that ultimate truth: *that I had a bus accident and that I'm nothing but a crippled girl inside an asylum, killing time by making up stories.*

In truth, there's not much sense in anything I am doing—or have done since I met the Pillar.

In truth, I could be just insane, and anyone who is listening to my rambling is only a victim of my bothered mind.

In truth, I could just accept all the madness around me, and laugh at it, like a morning cartoon on a TV screen—you get a few laughs, eat your cereal, and just totally forget about it.

I can just admit my madness and be fine with it. Lie back as the world spins like a cuckoo around my head.

But what always bothers me about my madness is that I know about it. I question it. I try to analyze it. Aren't mad people supposed to not know about themselves being mad?

My thoughts are interrupted by something all of a sudden. Something that connects the dots somehow. At least it moves things forward, just like our everyday lives when we don’t have an idea of what’s going on but hang on to the little clues we have for today.

What I see in front of me is the Snail Mound, the one the Hatter wanted me to find, and the March Hare warned me of.

Chapter 49

Meeting Hall, Buckingham Palace, London

Squeezed in a chair, among the big crowd in the hall, was Dr. Tom Truckle.

He had managed to fool the guards, pretending he was the person whom the invitation was originally for. It wasn't hard. He wore his best tuxedo and rented an expensive Bentley, and made Ogier pretend he was his private chauffeur.

Once he arrived at the palace, he pompously flashed his invitation and trotted inside.

He was led through dimly lit corridors, one after the other, until he reached a secret meeting hall somewhere inside the palace.

Then he was shown his seat without anyone realizing what an impostor he was.

In the dimmed hall, he couldn't see the many important men and women from all over the world who sat beside him. Was he really sitting among those people?

The stage itself was bright, awaiting the Queen's arrival. Dr. Tom Truckle waited with anticipation to know what the heck this Event was about.

Chapter 50

Wonderland

Time remaining: 9 hours, 44 minutes

Stunned, I try to think it over. So the Hatter thought the Snail Mound was in the Garden of Cosmic Speculation in the real world, but it's actually in Wonderland?

It seems plausible to me, since the Hatter seems ignorant of how to get to the circus.

Let's rethink this, Alice. You're here, mainly to catch a rabbit before it explodes, but to do that you have to play the Hatter's game by finding the circus. That's all you know about this. STOP analyzing and go find the circus.

I run barefoot toward the Snail Mound. It's a spiral mountain, like inverted cones with green roads upward until you reach its tip. It reminds me of a picture I once saw of Babylon, but I'm not sure if the two images are related.

I climb and climb in wide circles, wondering what I'll find at the top. Now it reminds me of Jack and the Beanstalk.

The spiral Snail Mound is huge. I am starting to pant, and I'm starting to feel weaker, but I keep going. It's surprising that the spiral movement wears off the induced Alice Syndrome. I am starting to see things in their normal size again.

In the end, when I reach the tip, I realize it's much smaller than I thought it was. A thought occurs to me suddenly: is it possible that Alice in the book never shrank, that she only was sick with Alice Syndrome, a scientifically known medical condition that may be caused by migraines?

Migraines? The kind Lewis Carroll suffered from? Is it possible that Lewis was ill? That his migraines drove him crazy? That he was just mad, like all of us?

I wash the nutty thoughts away, and focus on my climb.

It's really comforting seeing things as normal as they should be—not that many things about Wonderland *are* normal.

But it's beautiful from up here on the Snail Mound. It's like staring at a rainbow from the seventh sky, not from earth. Every curve in Wonderland is enchanting. I can easily spot the Queen's castle from here, and the Muffin Man's house, which I visited before.

The highest point on the Snail Mound is empty, except for my Tiger Lily bouncing to the sunlight on top.

"How did you get here?" I ask.

"I am always here." She snickers.

"No, you're not. You were down there a few minutes ago."

"Down there, up here, what does it matter?" She laughs. "As long as I have changed my mind to tell you about the circus."

I try to calm down and not lose it. "Why did you change your mind?"

"Frankly, because you found the Snail Mound."

"What does that mean?"

"The Snail Mound is only visible to three persons. That's

why the Hatter wanted you to find it for him."

"Oh." It makes a little more sense now. It doesn't explain the bomb in the rabbit and the dress, gloves, and fan, though. "Are you saying he is watching me now, that I am leading him to a place he shouldn't have access to?"

"It could be," she says. "I'm not the Hatter, you know."

Thinking about it, I still have no choice. I have to keep my deal with the Hatter so he'll tell me where the rabbit is. "You said only three persons can find the Snail Mound?"

"Lewis Carroll, the March Hare, and... guess what?" She winks.

"The Real Alice?" I am hoping.

"You're right about that."

"So it's me." I sigh. "Finally."

"Well, it's still a bit tricky," she says. "You see, you're the Real Alice in an unreal world."

"What do you mean?"

"I mean since you've fallen into the rabbit hole, you've been transported to this place, which, frankly—I'm not sure what it is. It could be a mimicking version of Wonderland, or anything else."

"I am not even registering anything you say." I hold my head tight to stop it from exploding. "Can you just tell me where the circus is?"

"It's right here in front of you," she says. "You came all the way up *here* to find something all the way down *there*." She points at Wonderland below.

I follow her gaze, and there it is in the distance: the circus's tent.

Chapter 51

Meeting Hall, Buckingham Palace, London

Dr. Tom Truckle watched the Queen take the stage.

People stood up and clapped enthusiastically as she embarked on a stepper to reach the podium. The smug smile on her face was prominent as she asked them to "shut up" and "sit down."

"Thank you for accepting my invitation for the most important event in the history of mankind," she began. "I have chosen you for reasons only the likes of *us* can understand. Each one of you has a past I sympathize with and understand clearly."

Dr. Tom thought he knew what she meant as he glanced at the list of members on the back of his card. But he needed to wait to confirm his suspicions.

"But before I lay out my plan, I'd like you to watch something." She signaled to Margaret Kent, and a screen came down behind her. "What you're going to see now will stir a few bad memories, but it's a must."

Dr. Tom watched the screen flicker, curious about what he was going to watch.

Chapter 52

The Maze, Wonderland

Time remaining: 9 hours, 23 minutes

It's quite a maze to get to the circus.

I tried to memorize it while I was atop the Snail Mound, but now I'm not sure I won't get lost down here.

It's a hedge maze, curving left and right, but I'm determined to finish it and get to the circus in the center—that's how it appeared to be from atop the spiral mound.

I notice that as I walk, the sky starts to turn blue again, and I seem to hear voices in the distance. The circus?

Hedge after hedge, curve after curve, I am going crazy. Whenever I think I am close to the sound, the maze ends.

I have to start all over again.

In my mind, I focus on the direction of the sound. Is it coming from my left side? Right side? Does it sound a bit muffled here because the maze is blocked? Does it flow better there?

The sounds are of a cheering crowd. Everyone seems happy about something. I am getting curiouser and curiouser.

More steps in, I stop in my tracks again.

Someone stands in front of me. Someone I didn't expect to see in here.

"Fabiola?"

"Nice to see you again, Alice." She is wrapped in white

from head to toe. Her dress flutters to a light breeze and her smile is ever so enchanting.

"I didn't expect to see *you* here," I say.

"I am not really who I am in this world, if that makes any sense."

"No. It doesn't make any sense." I chuckle feebly. "But what does?"

"I understand." She nods. "You're in the Bridge of Time between past and present, real and unreal. It's an aftermath of the March Hare trying to open portals to Wonderland with his gardens."

"So this isn't Wonderland?"

"It is... and it isn't."

"Here we go again," I mumble.

"It's like a memory where some things are true and some are lies." Fabiola is trying her best to make sense of it. "I have no idea how I am here, just like you. But I know *why* I am here."

"Why are you here, then, Fabiola?"

"To warn you. Whoever led you here with this maid's dress and asked you to seek the circus wishes you harm."

"What kind of harm?"

"The worst of all—emotional harm."

"Why does he want to harm me, whoever it is who's playing games?"

"It's the only way for you to remember—at least a few things."

"How I killed my friends in the bus?"

"No. That should come later," Fabiola says. "You're about to remember what really happened in the last days of Wonderland. Why the war is coming; a truth that I've tried to conceal for so long, even from myself."

"I thought Lewis Carroll locked the Wonderland Monsters in here, so they wouldn't bring chaos into the world," I say. "I saw him do it when I was in the Tom Tower. Isn't that Wonderland's biggest secret?"

"Not at all." Fabiola shakes her head. "Ever wondered why he locked them up?"

"I assumed they are evil." I try to think of a better word. "That they want to hurt people in the real world."

"That could be part of it, but it's not the real truth." Fabiola's eyes are watery. "You see, there is a reason why the Wonderland Monsters, led by the Queen of Hearts, are incredibly powerful."

"I had expected them to be led by the Cheshire," I say. "I mean, he seemed the most evil, with his power."

"The Cheshire is merely a hint to the dangers Wonderlanders could bring upon the real world. There is a reason why the Wonderland Wars could be the end of the world. A much grander reason," Fabiola says. "Ever wondered why the Cheshire hates humans so much?"

"Because humans killed his ancestors in an eye-rolling story I have never heard anything like before."

"That's hardly scratching the surface," Fabiola says. "Something happened to the Wonderland Monsters that made them this way—not that they weren't obnoxious in Wonderland, but the twist of evil in their personalities happened later."

"Why don't you spell it out for me, Fabiola? Why all the puzzles?"

"Because memories are mostly visual. You have to see them to remember—of course, that's if you're the Real Alice. I'm not going to go over this again."

"Apparently, this Hatter thinks I am her."

"We all hope you're her," Fabiola says. "I know I didn't believe it first, but trust me, I want to believe you're her. But I don't want to waste your time, as you have to go to circus and see what happened in the last days of Wonderland. I just wanted you to take notice of the door in the hedge to your right."

I turn my head and there it is. A wooden door I hadn't seen before.

"It's okay that you haven't seen it," she says. "Sometimes, when we're fixated on reaching the end, we miss the important things along the way."

"You want me to open it?"

"Not now," Fabiola says. "I'd prefer you open it on your way back. Its impact should be more to the point then."

I let out a long sigh. I'm tired. I am really tired. My mind is about to fry. If I just get one normal thought to hang on, I think I'll feel much better.

"I know it's hard." She steps over and touches my cheek. Her hands are warm. I feel at home. "And it's your choice to walk the distance or not. I mean, you could have just given up on a rabbit with a bomb threatening the children in London. A sane person would have done that."

"You mean only the insane walk the distance?"

"It's an unusual way to put it." She laughs. "But it's true. Insanity isn't always a curse. For those who know how to use it, it's a bliss. Now, I have to go, Alice."

She pulls her hand away and I feel lost. I feel without a family. Lonely, as usual.

I can hear the crowd in the distance cheering. Again, they sound so happy. I wonder how this could be bad at all.

"One more thing," Fabiola says. "Once you reach the end of maze, you won't be in Wonderland anymore. The Bridge of Time will take you to the 19th century."

"In the real world?"

"Yes." She nods. "The circus, Alice, was in the real world. It was the first moment in history when Wonderland and the real world collided."

Chapter 53

Meeting Hall, Buckingham Palace, London

Tom Truckle squinted at the screen in the dark.

The movie was out of this world. It was as if some loony director had made a movie about Wonderland, pushing everything up a notch. A great movie, indeed. Except that the Queen was calling it a documentary.

Everyone around Tom was sighing, and talking about how they missed the old days of Wonderland.

It should have driven him crazy, but it didn't. Tom, unbeknownst to most, was all too aware of Wonderland, and had his own plans for finding it.

Surely he had fooled everyone with his act, that he didn't believe that it existed—basically shocking Alice to death in the Mush Room for it—but that was all a facade.

No one really knew who he was, and he was just waiting for all the threads to come together so he could strike as hard as he planned.

But even so, watching this movie was melancholic.

What really took him by surprise was the part when the screen went black for a few seconds. Everything went silent, and then a word appeared on the screen.

A word that meant nothing to Tom, but stirred sighs among the crowd.

"And now," the Queen said, "it's time to look into this

memory we usually hate to remember, but trust me, it's a must."

The movie began, and Tom was wondering about that word he had just read. Why was it so frightening to everyone in the room, including the Queen?

It was a normal word. Even funny. A word that usually instilled mirth in the hearts of kids.

The word was: circus.

Chapter 54

The circus

Time remaining: 8 hours, 34 minutes

I run like a mad girl.

I think my feet are as curious as me, wanting to see the circus. It causes me to fall, but I pick myself up again, running in the maid's dress through the maze.

What could have happened in the circus? Why would the Wonderlanders have attended a circus? Did they work there?

Running, I imagine the Pillar as the circus ringmaster, using his wicked charm to lure kids into the tent. I imagine the Cheshire disguised as an evil clown. The March Hare, a mad knife thrower. Fabiola could be a ballerina, or a pantomime dancer luring people with the power of silence. The kids would love her. How about the rest? How about Jack?

Tears threaten to trickle down my face as I remember him. Is it possible he once lived with me in Wonderland?

I imagine us both working the trapeze. Alice Wonder, the trapeze girl, and Jack Diamond, the card magician. I imagine him climbing up the trapeze and catching me when I fall.

My mind is racing, as do my feet, as does my heart.

Suddenly, I am there. I finished the maze. I am in the center.

Slowing down, I am mesmerized by the fireworks in the sky, the crowd of families, and the endless supply of Wonderland food.

“Welcome to the circus.” A short ringmaster urges people inside. It’s not the Pillar. Someone I have never seen before. Just a normal man from the 19th century. “Please enter and see the wonders of the world!”

People start rushing inside while their kids lick on cotton candy. What could be so sinister inside? It looks so beautiful. A circus from about two centuries ago in the heart of...

Wait, is this still Scotland? London? I have no idea.

“Ladies and gentlemen, boys and girls, step inside, come closer,” the ringmaster calls out. “You will not believe your eyes. You won’t believe your mind.”

I approach in my maid’s dress, worried they won’t let me in, but a few kids push me through. Everyone is about to watch the anticipated show.

“Inside this tent, you will witness something you've never seen or heard before,” the ringmaster chirps. “It’s crazier than dreams, stranger than fiction.”

I am stepping inside.

The circus is beautiful. I notice it looks uncannily like the Six O’clock Circus in Mudfog Town, only this one is well taken care of. It’s huge!

“Welcome to the most amazing show on earth.” The ringmaster follows inside and steps in the ring. “Forget about magicians. Forget about clowns. Forget about trapeze girls.”

I sit among the enthusiastic crowd, wondering what the

show is going to be about. Why would you want to forget about clowns and magicians in a circus? What are we going to see, then?

And where are the Wonderlanders? I look around and see none of them.

"Ladies and gentlemen." The ringmaster raises his hands and the crowd is all seated now. "What you're about to see will blow your mind."

People clap all around me. I have a feeling this circus is famous. Either they have heard of it before, or have actually seen this show already.

"From America to Brazil, China to Europe, Africa to the North Pole," the ringmaster brags. "From all over the world, and now here for you in Britain. This is the show you all heard about." He waves his hand behind an ear, expecting the crowd to shout the name.

"The Maddest Show on Earth!" the crowd screams.

The ringmaster smiles, and calls two of his assistants to stand side by side next to him. A bald man and big woman, heavy on her feet. That's all I can see thus far.

"Are you ready?" he shouts.

The crowd's response is overwhelming.

Ready for what, I wonder.

All around him, men are putting a huge steel cage together while a few cute dancers entertain the crowd.

My heart is racing. What is the cage for? A lion?

“I suppose you all have your cotton candy with you.” The ringmaster smirks. “Because you will need it.”

All around me, people pull out bags of cotton candy in all colors.

I don’t know why but I’m starting to have a bad feeling about this. Fabiola was right. I don’t think I’m going to like what I will see, although I have no idea what to expect.

Why can’t I see any of the Wonderlanders?

“We’re close to starting the show,” the ringmaster says. The man and woman next to him look familiar. I squint, hoping I can recognize them. “But like every city and town we stop by, let me tell you about the show you’re about to see. Let me tell you about the Invisible Plague.”

Invisible Plague? I wonder what that could be.

As he finishes the sentence, I recognize the two people on his left and right. I can’t believe my eyes. I think I’m going to faint. It’s Waltraud and Ogier, my evil wardens at the Radcliffe Asylum.

Chapter 55

Meeting Hall, Buckingham Palace, London

"Before I resume the video, I have to remind you of what the circus was about," the Queen said, and Dr. Tom was listening eagerly. "What I want to remind you of is about something they used to call the Invisible Plague."

A few squeals escape the crowd. Tom too. He had heard about the Invisible Plague before, but thought it was only a myth. He stared back at the invitation card in his hand and read the list of the guests again, breathing heavily. This couldn't be.

"Back in the 18th and 19th centuries, when I lived in Wonderland, things were crazy," the Queen explained. "Crazy, but beautiful in a nonsensical way. The power of imagination Lewis Carroll had gifted us with had no boundaries. Animals and flowers talked. Endless parties where we threw teacups at each other—and loved it. And more. At some point, most of us could materialize their own thoughts into reality."

The crowd sighed.

"But then the hallucinations began, and things got weirder when that Alice girl entered our world, criticizing our mad ways of living. But who was she to understand the beauty of bonkers and borgroves of Wonderland?" the Queen said. "Let's not go into what damage she caused, and let's focus on the rabbit hole she created, the one that broke the realms between Wonderland and the silly human world."

Tom fidgeted in his seat. Didn't she say she was going to explain what the Invisible Plague was? He was curious.

"Humans began coming into our world, one by one," the Queen said. "And thus, we crossed over to their world, too. Suddenly, we found ourselves in a world we didn't belong to. A world of humans in the 19th century in London. Unlike the madly colorful Wonderland, their world was a place of war, poverty, and Victorian darkness."

The Queen stopped and ate a few of her favorite peanuts.

"Of course, humans' greatest weakness had always been their fear. In particular, the fear of others. They feared anything that was different from them so much that they had the audacity to kill it, exterminate it right away, and call it their enemy. To them, Wonderlanders were the maddest of the mad. At this time in history, insanity had not been medically explained yet, nor was it socially acceptable. Humans were as ignorant as those whom, of this world, call autistic children retarded. Humans were the worst creature the universe created."

Tom's perception of the Queen had been that of a total lunatic who longed for nothing but the obedience of others—like the flamingo in the asylum. Not that his perception of her had changed drastically now, but she wasn't as shallow as he'd thought. She actually had a story to tell. One that was going to blow his mind. He listened tentatively.

"So humans didn't just call us mad then," the Queen said. "They thought of us as a plague. And our plague, or disease, was an invisible one that affected our brains and had no well-known cure. Thus, the Invisible Plague."

Tom let out a sigh. Now his suspicion about the names of the people on the list was confirmed. Each and every one of them had been mad once. True, most of them were of notable prestige in their countries—senators, mayors, and even people who worked in the White House and the British Parliament. All of them had also been mad at some point in their lives.

How the government hired people who were once mad always boggled his mind.

Tom was sitting among more than two hundred mad lunatics from all over the world. Rich. Famous. Powerful lunatics.

"Now, you understand why I have summoned you to this meeting," the Queen said. "We're all the same, whether some of you were a Wonderlander once, or just labeled mad in this world." Her gaze intensified. "And you know what humans do to those of the Invisible Plague. You know what happens to you when you're called mad in this world."

Tom scratched his head. What was she talking about?

"I'm not talking about asylums and straitjackets," the Queen said. "I'm talking about the atrocities humans committed against those who needed help instead of being called 'mentally retarded.' I am talking about what humans have done to the likes of us in the past. I'm talking about the..."

She raised her hands in the air, and with them the crowd

stood up. The mad crowd from all over the world, saying the same words in unison, as if it were a ritual: “You’re talking about what happened to us in the circus.”

Chapter 56

The circus

Time remaining: 7 hours, 00 minutes

Before I can comprehend what Waltraud and Ogier are doing here, several people are pushed into the cage.

The crowd is screaming. I grit my teeth against their squeals. All of them stand up and clap, blocking my view.

I am going crazy. Who is in the cage below?

I try to look, but the crowd won't let me. Furiously, I jump outside the tier to the small aisles. I still can't see those in the cage, so I descend the rows barefoot, the image clearer with each step down.

This can't be true.

This can't be true.

This can't be true.

I see Lewis Carroll holding the bars of the cage from inside, pleading for mercy.

What is going on? I run faster.

Then I see Duchess Margaret Kent behind him. Everyone is booing and throwing cotton candy at her.

I run closer.

I see the Queen of Hearts, her hands cuffed as she screams at the crowd. Then I see the Muffin Man. The March Hare.

Oh my God. What's going on?

"Please don't," Lewis says to the crowd. "You don't

understand. They're just different. They won't hurt you."

I am a few steps away from the cage when I see Fabiola in the back, crying herself to death. Then there is Jack.

Jack!

I grip the cage. "What's going on, Jack?"

"You shouldn't be here, Alice," Jack shouts at me, cotton candy sticking to his face. "Run!"

"I won't run, Jack." The scene is overwhelming. I'm going to cry. I realize that almost everyone from Wonderland is inside the cage. "Tell me how I can help."

"Run, Alice!" Lewis yells. "Run!"

I turn and look at the supposedly sane people of the world, shouting and discriminating against those behind the cage. Men, women, and their children. Where in the world does such madness come from? Why do they hate them so much?

As answers form slowly in my cloudy head, the ringmaster spells it out for me.

"Look at those freaks!" he announces. "Aren't they funny? Aren't they amusing? Aren't they disgusting?"

Freaks? Is that what humans thought of the Wonderlanders when they crossed over to their world? Because they looked and acted differently?

"Those mad, mad, mad creatures!" the ringmaster says. "Hit them with your cotton candy. Laugh at that grinning cat. Amuse yourself with this short freak that thinks she's a queen. Entertain yourself with the silly jokes of the man with the hat who throws tea parties and always thinks it's six o' clock." He points at someone with a long hat. I can't see his face in the shadows, but I'm assuming he is the Mad Hatter.

Suddenly, the crowd is given teacups, and they start throwing them at the Mad Hatter.

They laugh at them.

My head veers between those thought of as mad, freaks in the cage, and those supposedly sane people throwing cups at them.

"Stop it!" I scream at the crowd. "Who the heck do you think you are? It's not them who're freaks. It's you!"

Then I realize my mistake.

Everything stops as they stare at me.

Chapter 57

Meeting Hall, Buckingham Palace, London

"It started as a joke," the Queen said. "At first, no one understood a person suffering from a mental disorder. Usually they thought those people were possessed by demons, causing to have those hallucinations. Then they thought of them as witches. In both cases, they were killed, if not burned at the stake."

Tom was sweating by now. Surely he sat among the maddest of the mad in the world, but the Queen was also reciting the true dark history of humans, which had been repeatedly documented—only historians always preferred to stay away from it.

People with a mental illness were used as a tourist attraction, a means for entertainment, all over the years.

In his office, Tom had a drawing of people watching mad people for entertainment.

"Then when physicians began suggesting this was an illness, calling it the Invisible Plague, humans came up with this humiliating idea of gathering the mad in a prison, as if they had committed a crime," the Queen explained. "And in a world were money dominates everything, there was nothing wrong with making a shilling or a buck on the side. The mad people were put into cages as a tourist attraction. People from all over the world would entertain themselves by watching them for a fee. It was like going to comedy movie."

Tom reached for his pills and swallowed. A handful. Everything the Queen had talked about, he knew for a fact.

"So we, mad people, Wonderlanders, instead of being cured, were a source of a few laughs and snickers," the Queen said. "We became the freaks in the circus." She signaled for her mad crowd to sit again. "And now it's time we have our revenge." She clicked her remote and the screen flickered again.

It was time to see what she had on her mind.

Chapter 58

The circus

Time remaining: 6 hours, 47 minutes

I stand, staring at the crowd in the circus with my heart pounding in my feet. What are they going to do to me?

When I think of it, the only real human in the cage is Lewis Carroll. Still, they didn't spare him. Of course, because he was defending the Wonderlanders—so Lewis didn't always just think of them as monsters?

I assume they will do the same to me now.

Caught between running and saving those in the cage, I realize this is some sort of a memory. It's doubtful I can change much about it. Whoever led me here wanted me to just see this.

Why? I have no idea.

Maybe he wants me to sympathize with Black Chess and their crimes in the real world.

I am confused. Who's mad and who isn't?

Those who turned evil after what happened to them in the cage, or those people throwing cotton candy at those poor souls?

"Run!" Fabiola shouts.

Her voice reminds me of the room she wanted me to see back in the maze.

I turn around and run, tears filling my eyes. On my way out, teacups smash all around me.

The way back into the maze seems easier. I think I know

my way, and I wonder if any of those in the circus will follow me here.

As I run, I try to connect the dots.

So when I saw Lewis Carroll lock the Wonderland Monsters behind the doors of Wonderland, was he protecting the world from them, or protecting them from the world?

Fabiola said the circus happened in the last days before he locked them in, so it's safe to think he was protecting them. Or maybe he was protecting some and locking up others.

I like this assumption better, because apparently not all of those in the cage turned out to be part of Black Chess. Fabiola isn't, for instance. The event at the circus had a different effect on each of them.

Also, I am not sure why I haven't seen the Pillar, but I could have missed him in all this mess.

Panting, I reach the door.

I turn the knob and step into a room where people are gathered around a meal in Lewis Carroll's studio.

The image brings instant tears to my eyes, and I fight the weakness in my body that's bringing me down to my knees.

Chapter 59

Meeting Hall, Buckingham Palace, London

Dr. Tom Truckle watched the Queen's video with intent. It was hard to predict where this was going, but the crowd around him was shocked.

It seemed strange for a man like him to sympathize with the mad, but he did—at least momentarily.

He kept watching the video, eagerly wanting to know what the Queen had on her mind. What kind of revenge was she talking about? How did the mad have their revenge?

The video he was watching detailed what had happened to the Queen and Wonderlanders in the circus. The torture, the humiliation, and the human race's fear of what was different or new to them.

Even Tom, a man who rarely sympathized with the insane, hated his own kind for the few moments he watched what had happened to the Wonderlanders.

Chapter 60

Behind the Door, the Maze, on the borders of Wonderland

Time remaining: 6 hours, 11 minutes

The people gathered inside Lewis Carroll's studio are my friends. Those who, according to Fabiola, walked the white tiles on the Chessboard of Life.

"Alice!" Lewis cheers with a glass of wine in his hand. He is sitting at the head of a table filled with all kinds of colorful food. The place looks cozy, like how you would expect your family's house to look.

To his right sits Fabiola, nodding and smiling at me. "We missed you, Alice. I thought we'd wait for you to say prayers before we began eating."

I step closer and wipe the tears from my eyes. Is this room some sort of a dream?

A dream within a dream? A madness within hallucinations?

"You have to taste those vegetables," says the March Hare, looking as sane and relaxed as he ever has. "I grew them myself in my garden."

I am starting to assume this isn't a dream. I think the door transported me to another time, maybe before the circus, when life seemed peaceful in Wonderland.

Those at the table may be all the friends I had at this time.

"Missed you, Alice!" A younger girl, next to Fabiola,

waves at me. She has a cute smile, but I don't recall meeting her before.

I wave back and approach the table.

"The best chicken soup in Wonderland," a voice says behind me. It's Jack. He brings a bowl of soup filled with playing cards to the table and sits next to the March Hare. "Come sit, girl."

I sit opposite Lewis Carroll, wondering when this really happened. But in any case, I'm glad, because this means I am *her*. I am the Real Alice, right?

We start all holding hands, and Fabiola asks me to say a prayer again.

"I don't know any," I say.

"Just say what's on your mind," Lewis says. "We're family now. We'll accept what you feel inside your heart."

Overwhelmed by the possibility of having had such a family at some time, overwhelmed by this peace and love, I stare at Fabiola's angelic, motherly smile, Lewis' fatherly care, the little girl's innocence, and Jack's loving eyes. The March Hare could simply fit as good uncle who takes care of us as much as his garden.

My phone rings suddenly. I pick it up while everyone glares at me. Not even Carroll imagined such a device in his time—I guess I will have to explain it to them later.

But there may be no later.

The message is from the Hatter, not the one I saw in the

circus, but the one from real life:

Thank you for telling me the circus's whereabouts; no one would have found it but you.

And, oh, all of this you see happened once in the past, Alice. Enjoy the very short moment, as it will turn upside down right now. Enjoy a glimpse of Wonderland as it was so long ago.

You led me to the circus, and I have to thank you for that. This is why I showed you this intimate moment of your past through this portal.

I raise my head to the questioning friends on the table, but I have to type back now, and explain later:

You got what you wanted. The location of the circus, although I don't know why it's so important. I need the location of the rabbit. You promised.

The response arrives sooner than I expected:

Go to the Six O'clock Circus in real life. You will find a device buried underneath the sand in the ring. The device can locate the rabbit's every move. Good luck. Now, I leave with the last tragedy in the scene.

P.S. You will never find the rabbit if you're not wearing the dress. And, ah, again, the fan and gloves you found are the wrong ones. But don't worry, you should find them, and understand their importance, once you find the rabbit.

Find the rabbit, save the world, and find out who you really are.

I tuck my phone back in my pocket, and smile at my

family. "I'll explain what this is later."

"Is that from the future?" The March Hare raises a thick eyebrow.

"Kinda."

"Kinda?" Jack asks. "What does *kinda* mean?"

"Ah." I sigh. "That's a long story. Should I say the prayers now?"

"Please do." Lewis and Fabiola exchange smiles and stare at me. I don't know what it means, but suddenly I realize they maybe were a couple one day.

I grip Jack's hand harder on my left, and this cute younger girl on my right, and begin...

But like the Hatter said, *it won't last long*.

The door bursts open. Victorian police dash in and arrest Fabiola, Jack, March Hare, and the girl on account of being infected with the Invisible Plague.

Lewis stands and defends them. The police knock him down and take him along. "You're infected, just like all of them," the constable roars, and hits him on the back. "You all shall die before you infect the rest of the world."

I realize that this memory is the last of the happy ones for the six of us.

As for me, I feel like I am fading away, melting between the sheets of insanity, returning with my body and soul to the place where I originally started. The place people like to call the real world. Sometimes, they call it the sane world.

Chapter 61

The Garden of Cosmic Speculation, Scotland

Time remaining: 5 hours, 04 minutes

I wake up in the rabbit hole again. Dirt surrounds me everywhere.

Whatever this trip was, I have no idea. But I know I learned a lot.

A lot!

A tiny slant of light peers through from above. Someone is unlocking the hole.

"Alice." The Pillar peeks inside. "Can you hear me?"

"Yes."

"We finally found you. We seemed to miss the hole before. It's strange. I don't know how it happened," the Pillar says. "Hang tight. We're sending someone to pick you up now."

"Pillar," I say, "until they pull me out, you should prepare the plane. I have to go back to the Six O'clock Circus."

"Why? What's there?"

"Trust me, I know much more than you do right now."

Chapter 62

Six O'clock Circus, Mudfog Town, on the Outskirts of London

Time remaining: 3 hours, 07 minutes

I am back in the Six O'clock Circus, where it all started. The Pillar is watching me while I crawl on hands and knees and dig into the sand where the Piccadilly writing had been embedded before.

I dig everywhere for that device the Hatter told me about. I have to find it. Time is running out.

"Will you ever talk to me?" the Pillar says. "I've been begging you all the way here on the plane. What's gong on, Alice?"

"I have to find a device that will locate the rabbit so I can stop the bomb." I am still digging like a mad rabbit. "It's buried in the sand."

"And I suppose the Hatter told you this somehow while you were in the hole in the Garden of Cosmic Speculation?"

"Yes. It's a long story."

"Why don't you tell me about it?" he says. "Because there was nothing inside that hole. It was just a *hole*. We couldn't even find a rabbit."

"Are you questioning my sanity now?" I snap.

The Pillar sighs.

"Because I am certified, you know. The beauty of it is I can do and believe whatever I want."

"You're not making sense, Alice. Let's slow down."

"Sense?" I am on the verge of shouting. "What has ever made sense since I met you? Just shut up and let me find the device." Inside, I want to cry. Why? Because he is right. Nothing makes sense. Even if some of the events made little sense before, I'm too deep into the rabbit hole of absurdity to recall such events.

But somehow, I keep chugging my way through. God only knows where it will lead me.

"Okay, I admit I may have been insensitive," the Pillar says. I wonder why he isn't sarcastic at the moment. Why is he so serious about wanting to know what happened in the hole? It's not like him. "Just tell me about the rabbit hole in the Garden of Cosmic Speculation. What happened in there?"

"It's a portal to Wonderland."

"Are you saying you were in Wonderland?" The Pillar seems eager to know.

"Not quite so." I shrug. "It's part Wonderland, part real world, part time machine." I am well aware of how impossible this sounds, but I trust in what I saw. I trust my mind—ironically, I do.

"Hmm..." The Pillar rubs his chin.

"Look, you're supposed to be the one who always believes me, the one who always encourages me to save lives." I stand up. "So don't go *hmm* on me."

"I'm not. I am only wondering why you're not really telling what you saw."

"You want to know what I saw?" The tension in my arms seems to be an aftermath of the horrific scene of the circus where the Wonderlanders where humiliated. It seems as if it all starts to sink in now. And it's too much to take. "I saw the circus!"

The Pillar grimaces. It's like I have stuffed him inside a pinball machine and kicked him all around.

"I saw the real circus. The Invisible Plague. I saw what humans, the likes of me, did to the Wonderlanders, only because they were different." I am shivering. "Is that what the Wonderland Wars are all about, Pillar? Is that why there's a Wonderland Monsters plan to destroy every living human? Why haven't you told me about it? Why have you lied to me?"

I hate it that tears stream down my face. I hate them.

But the image of Lewis, Fabiola, Jack, the girl, and the March Hare being taken by the British constables and sent to the circus shattered me. The image of humans rejecting anyone who is different from them makes me hate my own kind.

"I didn't know how to explain such a horrific thing to you," the Pillar says. He looks saddened. Surprisingly ashamed. "You wouldn't have believed me. No one would have believed me. It's a fact, buried deep down in the tombs of history books, deep down in the conscience of mankind. Something no one wants to talk about anymore. I mean, lining up mentally ill persons behind a cage for entertainment, as if they were animals in a zoo? Who would have believed me?"

"But you lied to me and told me Lewis locked the Wonderland Monsters in Wonderland."

"I didn't lie. It's true. Some of them he managed to lock in Wonderland, and some he managed to give new identities in the real world, like Fabiola," the Pillar says. "It was complicated. On one hand, humans tortured Wonderlanders, so he was trying to protect us all from them. And on the other hand, Wonderlanders, like the Cheshire, a victim of human atrocities too many times, had become a clear threat to the world. I don't even think Lewis knew what he was doing."

"And now what?" I say. "How do you expect me to hunt the Wonderland Monsters knowing what we humans have done to them? Do you have any idea how confused I am?"

"A monster is a monster." He grabs my arms tightly. "No matter the circumstance that turned them into one."

"Coming from you, a man who killed twelve innocent people." I push him away.

"Forget about me. Don't you see what's happening here? Whoever showed you the circus wanted you to think that way." The Pillar grits his teeth. "They want you to sympathize with the Wonderland Monsters."

I realize his remark is right on the money. It may explain what most of this was about. This Hatter, probably on good terms with the Queen of Hearts and the Cheshire, wants me to feel for them, if not join them against the world.

Could it be this Hatter is actually the Cheshire?

As I think, my feet hit a bulge in the sand. I kneel down and see something protruding from it. I dig again.

Here it is.

A small, round thing, like a compass, but with a black digital screen. A red dot shimmers on the far left of it. “Here it is." I show it to the Pillar. "The rabbit's location. I need to go there now."

The Pillar takes a moment, staring at it. His face dims a little.

"What now?" I say.

"I'm just wondering what the rabbit is doing in your house, where we were yesterday.”

Chapter 63

Buckingham Palace, London

As he was getting ready to enter the meeting hall after a small break for coffee and cakes, Dr. Tom Truckle still couldn't believe he was standing among those important people from all over the world.

None of them were presidents, or prime ministers, but they were close, mostly friends of presidents and prime ministers.

What was the Queen planning to do with them? And how come they'd all lived in Wonderland once?

Tom avoided any prolonged conversations, so he wouldn't blow his cover. After all, he hadn't been truly invited. He was just an imposter in this party, the same way the Queen of Hearts was, posing as if she were the real Queen of England.

How did she even do this? And what did she do to the poor Queen of England?

The idea that Britain was now ruled by a queen from Wonderland drove him crazy. This was the kind of stuff his patients said in the asylum. The kind of the stuff he sent them to the Mush Room for.

Tom heard them announce the end of the break. It was time to get back in and listen to the Queen's final words. Time to listen to her telling them what this meeting was really for.

As he strolled back, he reminded himself that each person on the invitation list had been, at least once, convicted of madness.

Chapter 64

Alice Wonder's house, 7 Folly Bridge, Oxford

Time remaining: 1 hours, 44 minutes

When Edith opens the door for me, she looks like she has seen a ghost, again. I guess she didn't expect my return, not in a million years. But I had to. My device is flashing red in my hand. The rabbit with the bomb is somewhere in my childhood house.

"You got some nerve." Edith groans. She has two spots swelling in her head, from when she fell down after I hit her. They're red, and make her look like a devil.

I push her aside and let myself in, following the lead from my device. "I need to get in. There is something inside that I am looking for."

Waving her fan, Lorina descends the stairs and looks at me with wide eyes. "Are you serious?" She tilts her head between me and Edith. "Are you freakin' serious?"

"She thinks the rabbit is in here." Edith closes the door behind me and laughs.

"See? Now I know you two are hiding something," I say. "I never told you about that. How do you know about the rabbit? The police never spread the word about it to keep the people from going crazy."

"You're really nuts," Lorina says. "I mean, I'm going to call the asylum to come and get you now."

"Listen," I say. "All I need is the rabbit, and I promise you will never see me again. Not that I would want to see any of you again after what happened here the last time."

As the two sisters mock me, I stare at my device. It says I am standing in the right spot. The rabbit should be right under my feet, but there is nothing there. "Where are you hiding it?" I ask them. "How come you're involved in all of this? I am really losing my mind."

"You lost that a long time ago." Lorina chuckles. "How about another round of None Fu?"

"I'm not joking," I say. "Time is really running out and there is a rabbit with a bomb in this house."

"Not in this house, dear mad sister." Edith turns the TV on. "The rabbit is all over the city."

I stare at the TV and see someone has leaked the news of a loose rabbit with a bomb inside. People all over London are going bonkers looking for it. Streets blocked, others shut down, in a frantic search for the rabbit. Other people catch all the rabbits they can and lock them in a cage on the back of a huge truck, preparing to drive out of the city before the deadline.

The whole city of London has gone mad.

Chapter 65

Alice Wonder's house, 7 Folly Bridge, Oxford

Time remaining: 1 hours, 30 minutes

"How is that possible? Who leaked the news?" I ask.

"That mysterious man who calls himself the Hatter was on TV an hour ago," Lorina says. "Just like the Muffin Man last week. Living in London is starting to feel like a curse."

"But the rabbit is here." I stare back at the device in my hand. "It has to be here. The Hatter gave me this device. What's the point in fooling me again?"

Edith laughs. "Poor sis, can't you get it?" She approaches me. "Whoever is playing this game with you doesn't care about the rabbit. Haven't we warned you before?"

"What do you mean?"

"Whoever is playing this game with you is playing it with us too." Lorina shows me a message on her phone. It's from an anonymous number, saying they know about the Event.

"The Event?" I grimace.

"We used to call it the circus," Edith says.

A big lump is struck in my throat. "You know about the circus, too?"

"Oh." Lorina faces Edith. "So this Hatter must have shown her, or told her, about the circus, too."

"This is getting on my nerves," Edith says. "I wonder what he has on his mind. Why is he doing this?"

"Wait, you two!" I shout. "What are you saying? How do you know about the circus?" Then a thought strikes me. "Are you two from Wonderland, too?"

Now both my sisters really laugh.

"No, darling." Edith pats me, but not in a kind way. "Wonderland isn't real. It only exists in your *franjous* mind." She laughs louder. "Lorina and I are real people. We are from the real world."

"But, of course, we still know about the circus." Lorina grins, as if intentionally wanting to drive me mad.

I grit my teeth, collect what's left from the fragments of my thoughts, and pretend I'm the most logical person on earth. "Let's go over this again. Are we both talking about the same circus?"

"The one where mad Wonderlanders were kept in a cage by humans and made fun of?" Edith's grin widens. "Then yes, we're talking about the same circus."

I have no idea how she knows that.

"The same circus where people had the Invisible Plague." Lorina waves her fan. "Yes, loony sis, we know about that."

"But how is that possible?" I say. "How could you not believe in Wonderland and believe in the circus in the same instant?"

"You really want to know?" Edith looks at my device flashing red.

I nod.

"Are you sure?" Lorina says. "I mean, you seem to have forgotten all about it somehow."

"Forgotten about it?"

"Yes, forgotten about our greatest secret," Lorina says. "Me, you, and Edith—Mother included, too."

"What secret?" I find myself taking a step away from them. It's as if I am close to remembering something, but my mind is resisting it.

The haze in my mind returns, and I realize that's a sign of remembering the things I fear to remember. It's been the same all day long. Whenever I felt dizzy or saw that haze, I was unconsciously resisting the truth about my past.

"You know where your device is pointing at?" Lorina says, sounding too sure of herself.

"It's supposed to point at the rabbit."

"That's what the Hatter wants you to think," Edith says. "We have no idea why he wants to lead you down this road, but we don't care, because it's time for us to remind you about what really happened in the circus."

And I thought I had seen enough—remembered enough.

"The device is pointing to the right spot," Lorina explains. "Only it's not the rabbit, but the basement underneath your feet."

"The basement?"

"Yes." Edith grins. "Want to go down there to remember our secret?"

I know I shouldn't say yes, but curiosity definitely killed

the cat. And I’m starving for any real truth about my past, even from my hating sisters.

“Good girl,” Lorina says. “Let’s go.” She glances at Edith. “By the way, the maid’s dress looks so good on you, Alice.”

I have a feeling I am going to understand what she is implying in a few minutes.

Chapter 66

Alice Wonder's house, 7 Folly Bridge, Oxford

Time remaining: 1 hours, 12 minutes

Descending to the basement, I see Edith putting on her gloves. And with Lorina's fan, I realize those are the fan and the gloves I was supposed to find.

Then I remind myself I am wearing the maid's dress. The triangle is complete. The three things the Hatter had wanted me to find, only I mistook the fan and gloves I found in the bottom drawer in my room upstairs for Lorina's fan and Edith's gloves.

What kind of truth am I about to know about my past? I have a feeling it's going to be darker than darkness itself.

There is a small cage in the basement, a smaller version of the one I saw in Wonderland. Toys are scattered all over the floors. Endless books, dog-eared and ripped apart, are scattered on the floor. All of them copies of *Alice in Wonderland.*

Closer, I see countless playing cards and chess pieces in the corners, too. What happened in this room?

"Still can't remember?" Edith folds her arms in front of her.

"I'd prefer if you tell me." I shrug. My own suppressed memories are on the tip on my tongue.

"This was your circus," Lorina says. "We used to cage you in here when you were seven years old."

I try not to panic. I think it's coming back to me.

"We used to make all kinds of fun of you," Edith says without the slightest tinge of guilt in her voice. "Sometimes we invited our friends from school to watch you in the cage."

"We let them watch you with your silly books, playing cards, and, of course, those stupid Lewis Carroll childhood tales," Lorina says.

"It was fun," Edith says. "Of course, we only did it when Mum was away, trying to make a living after Father left."

"And you never said a word to Mum," Lorina whispers in my ear. "You know why?"

"Why?" My hands are trembling.

"Because you were a coward, among so many other reasons."

"What was the point of keeping me in a cage and entertaining your friends?" I ask, my lips dry, my neck feeling wobbly.

"You were mad, Alice," Edith says. "It was so much fun having a mad member of the house."

"With all your funny stories about Wonderland," Lorina elaborates. "The white rabbits, the Hatter and the tea parties, and don't get me started with 'eat me' cake."

"It seemed like you read everything in the Alice books and thought they happened to you, only you made them more sinister," Edith explains. "Lorina and I had always been the bullies in school. It was so much fun, but we had no one to make fun of when we got back home."

"And there was you." Lorina snickers. "The highlight of every day."

"I was seven years old, for God's sake." A tear trickles down my cheek. A blurry memory of me holding on to the cage, begging to be let go, attacks me.

"But you were really entertaining," Lorina says. "That Invisible Plague of yours. Oh, man."

Suddenly, a question hits me. "How do you know about the Invisible Plague? How did the idea of the cage come to you?"

Lorina and Edith stare at each other, suppressing a bubbly laugh. Then they let it out in a burst of chuckles and snickers.

"Alice. Alice. Alice." Lorina wraps her threatening arms around me. "You were the one who gave us the idea."

Chapter 67

Buckingham Palace, London

The Queen of Hearts, posing as the Queen of England, was ready to take the stage again. She was about to go announce her brilliant plan after showing her guests one last video.

But she couldn't do it before she received that call she was waiting for.

Her phone rang.

"What took you so long?"

"A few twists and turns in my plan," a muffled voice said. "But it'll be good in a few minutes."

"So the video will be ready?"

"Give it half an hour," the voice said. "I'm on it. It will be a live feed, and you will be able to show it to your guests."

"Is it going to be good enough?"

"Much more than you think," the voice said. "A piece of art, like nothing you ever seen."

"Frabjous." She grinned, feeding Brazilian nuts to one of her dogs. "Everyone in Britain is going nuts looking for the rabbit with the bomb. I can't pretend I didn't hear about it much longer. The public will need some statement. But I can't wait half an hour to show the surprise to my guests."

"You will, My Queen," the voice said. "Long live Wonderland. Death to the real world."

"Ah, one more thing," the Queen said. "Next time, I prefer

you tell me your plans in detail. When Margaret first told me about the rabbit loose in the streets, you hadn't told me this was your plan. I stood oblivious of what was going on."

"Apologies, My Queen," the voice said. "The idea came out of the blue, after I learned of a psychological term called the Rabbit Hole."

"Really? Is that a real scientific term?"

"Just like the Alice Syndrome," the voice said. "It seems those real-world doctors stole their ideas from Lewis Carroll's genius interpretations. The Rabbit Hole means putting a patient under severe stress, metaphorically sending them into a rabbit hole, and pushing until they remember their past."

"Well done, then," she said. "So I should be counting on her remembering?"

"Like I said, it's only half an hour and she will remember," the voice said. "However, it will be most heart-wrenching. I am making sure she doesn't die or something from the shock."

"We can't afford this girl to die, you know that."

"Don't worry," the voice said. "I have it under control."

"And her sisters?"

"They know nothing," the voice said. "They are just pawns in the game. Doing what I have planned for them to do."

Chapter 68

Alice Wonder's house, 7 Folly Bridge, Oxford

Time remaining: 1 hour, 01 minutes

"How did I give you the idea?" I ask, as flashes of my horrible childhood are nothing but playing cards flying in front of my eyes. I can't seem to catch any of the cards to take a better look, but I see fragments, flashes, flipping before my eyes.

Flashes of who I really am.

"This brings is us to the shocking truth." Lorina waves her fan again. The memory of her waving it and snickering while Edith punches with her gloves while I am inside the cage hits me like a plague. Now I know what the gloves and fan meant. But what is the dress for?

"Are you telling me there is a more shocking truth than what you have just told me?" My breathing grows heavier. First I witness the atrocities against Wonderlanders in the circus, then my own horrible childhood in the basement of my family's house, then I am supposed to learn something much darker?

"Remember when we told you went missing as a seven-year-old girl?" Lorina says. "Remember when we told you, you told us about having gone to Wonderland and came back with that glinting knife in your hand?"

I nod, but don't say a word.

"That actually never happened that way," Edith says. "The truth is..." She hesitates. "That you were never lost."

“What happened then?” I ask.

“Alice.” Lorina stares right into my eyes. “You knocked on our door one day. When we opened it you were a lost seven-year-old standing with a knife in her hand, blood spattered all over.”

“I—I am not following.”

“I wanted to kick you out, but Mother took sympathy on you,” Edith says. “I mean, I never understood why she wanted to save you.”

“She is my mother,” I retort. “Of course she’d want to save me.”

“She doesn’t get it, yet,” Lorina told Edith. “You think we shouldn’t tell her?”

I scream at them, “Tell me what?” Deep inside, I have already remembered the truth. “Tell me what, Edith?” I shake her with all my might.

Edith doesn’t reply. I think she enjoys the madness lingering in my eyes.

I find myself turning around, looking for something to threaten them with. Funny—or terrifying—how my eyes spot a glinting knife on the floor right away. I kneel down, grab it, stand up, and press them both against the wall. “Tell me what?”

“That’s the same look you had in you eyes when you were seven years old,” Lorina says.

“Tell me what, goddammit?”

“That you knocked on our door, told us you were running

from the Wonderland Monsters, that they wanted to kill you, that something horrible happened in Wonderland."

"You were laughable," Edith continues. "A lost, mad child whom my mother pitied and took in and made you one of us."

"You mean...?"

"You were never our sister, Alice," Lorina says, as if she is delivering the happiest news in her life. "You were never one of us, and you have always been mad."

Chapter 69

Buckingham Palace, London

Tom Truckle saw the Queen of England take the podium, that sinister grin glinting like a knife on her face.

"Ladies and gentlemen," she said. "Pardon me, I mean *mad* ladies and gentlemen." She snickered and the crowd laughed. "I am about to offer you something that hasn't been done in the history of mankind before. Something that will make us, Wonderlanders and fellow madmen and women, avenge what happened to us in the circus two centuries ago."

Tom noticed the glaring silence of the crowd. Everyone seemed to be counting on the Queen now.

"What we're going to do is going to shake this human world upside down," she said. "It will make Wonderland look like such a very sane place to what we're going to do to the real world around us."

Tom himself was as anxious as ever. Although an imposter, he felt like he'd like to be part of the Queen's lunatic plan. Who worked in an asylum and didn't feel like the sane world outside wasn't the enemy. To Tom it was the taxes he paid, the expenses of his divorce, and his medications. How much did he have to pay for those pills, just to stay sane in this mad world?

"But first, I want to show you a glimpse of the kind of madness you love to watch." She pointed at the screen behind her. It showed people in England hunting all kinds of rabbits, opening them up to look for a bomb. Some people killed the rabbits, some ran when they saw one, even if it was on TV. The streets were a mess of accidents and panic. And oh, how insane the world looked right now. "This is just the beginning. In a few minutes you will be watching something much more insane, so keep watching."

Chapter 70

Alice Wonder's house, 7 Folly Bridge, Oxford

Time remaining: 53 minutes

"That's why you hate me so much." I nod at Lorina and Edith. "I never was one of you."

In truth, I can't remember the part of me knocking on their door with a knife in my hand. But I do remember the basement. The horrible circus inside the basement.

"We don't just hate you, Alice. We loathe you," Lorina says. "You're like that itch in the top of my mouth that hurts more if I try to lick it away."

"Even when you were put in the asylum, you still escape and make our life miserable," Edith says, totally neglecting that I may have been just a troubled seven-year-old, but that the incidents in the basement—which were their fault—may have turned me into a loon.

"So how did you come up with the circus idea in the basement?"

"Because you told us about the circus in Wonderland," Lorina says. "Or rather the silly idea that Wonderlanders had crossed over to the real world in the 19th century, and that humans thought of them as mad people and freaks, and sent them to the circus for entertainment."

"Of course." I sigh. "That was how I gave you the idea. So you decided to take it up a notch and make a circus out of me in the basement."

"And it was fun, Alice," Edith says. "I mean, if you bully someone in the real world you may get in trouble. But bully a mad girl, wow, that was a million-dollar idea we got away with.

"Because whatever you were going to say about it, no one was going to believe a lost mad girl who thinks she came from Wonderland." Edith and Lorina high-five.

The Pillar comes to mind instantly. All his madness, theories, and the harsh ways he treats the people in this world seem just now. How I would like to choke both of them with a hookah's hose right now. Maybe I was hard on the Pillar. Maybe the twelve people he killed were the likes of Lorina and Edith. Bullies who needed to be put to rest.

In the same time I stand, contemplating my past and what to do with Edith and Lorina, I realize I am too late again. Why do I always waste time lamenting my true past?

Edith tugs on her gloves and picks up a baseball bat from the floor, while Lorina shoots me an even more sinister look now.

"How about we play that circus game one more time?" she says.

"What?" I grimace, unable to comprehend their thirst for evil.

"Come on, Mary Ann." Edith plops the bat against her fatty palm.

"What did you just call me?" I take a calculated step back. I was going to lash my None Fu at them when Edith caught me off guard with what she just said.

"Mary Ann." Lorina sticks out her tongue and shakes her head like a bully teasing a kid on school grounds. "Mary Ann."

"Why are you calling me Mary Ann?" I am fully aware that this is one of my names in the *Alice in Wonderland* book, that the rabbit mistakes me for a Mary Ann in the first chapter. But why do they call me by that name now?

What does it mean?

"Oh." Edith nudges me with the bat in my shoulder. Lorina fans away. "We didn't tell you?"

Both of my evil stepsisters wink at each other.

"You also held a pot next to the glinting knife the day you showed up on our door," Lorina says, still forcing me to step back, closer to the cage's opening behind me. "A pot with a tiger lily in it."

"Remember that pot, loony tunes?" Edith swooshes the bar a breath away from my nose. "Inside the pot, there was a necklace, which probably was yours."

"It belongs to someone called Mary Ann," Lorina says. "My mother called you Mary Ann then, and you never minded. It was only later when she realized your obsession with *Alice in Wonderland* that she called you Alice. She thought it sounded better for your adoption papers."

"And she gave you our last name, Wonder," Edith says. "Odd how it all fell into place, isn't it? Our last name being

'Wonder' while you think you came from Wonderland." This part seems to amuse her the most.

"So I was really Mary Ann in Wonderland?" I mumble.

"Here she goes again," Lorina tells her sister. "Did you see how bonkers she went, talking to herself about Wonderland again?"

"That's why we need to see her in the cage one more time." Edith pushes me harder, the cage against my back now. "Come on, Mary Ann. Entertain us one last time."

Edith's push does something to me. Something I was looking for all along: I remember them torturing me in the basement now. Vividly.

It's an even worse memory than remembering the Mush Room torture. The humiliation. Their friends they invited over to laugh at me. The worst memory a person can relive.

But one thing strikes me the most. In that memory I'm gripping something behind my back. Something I don't want them to see. I can feel it in my hand. It's cold. And small.

"Get in the cage!" Edith roars now.

I close my eyes and don't respond to her. My closed eyes are the draped curtain of my theatre of life, but they also open up another place in my memory when I was seven years old.

What was I holding in my hand back then that was important to me?

I can remember I didn't care about the pain. I only cared about that thing I was gripping.

What was it?

Then I remember seeing buckets in the corner of the room. A lot of cleaning tools next to them. What did I do with those buckets?

Risking the loss of my precious memory, I open my eyes, seeing if the buckets are still in the corner of the room right now.

They are!

Something inside me tells me I hid that precious thing in the back of my head in one of the buckets. Something tells me that this is what all this is about.

I am supposed to find what's in the bucket.

Edith and Lorina freak out when I aggressively beeline through them toward the buckets. I pull them out of the corner and rummage through them, having no idea what I am looking for, but knowing I will recognize it when I see it.

"What?" Lorina says behind me. "You missed your buckets, Mary Ann?"

"My buckets?" I turn back. "They are mine? Did they mean something to me?"

"The whole world." Edith rolls her eyes.

"What do you mean?" I insist. "Why did I have them?" I can't tell them about what I think I hid inside, because I'm somehow sure they shouldn't know about it.

If only I could remember it clearer now. If only!

"Here." Lorina holds a broom with the tips of her hand. "Yuck. Hold this." She gives it to me.

The broom is old. I don't know why it should mean anything to me. "What is this?" I shout then take a step forward and almost choke Lorina with one hand. "Tell me what's going on. What do these buckets mean to me?"

"They were—" Lorina is choking under my grip, so I turn to Edith.

"They were tools," Edith says.

"Tools for what?"

"Cleaning tools, duh!" Edith says. "Let my sister go."

I do. I loosen my grip, and Lorina slumps to the floor.

But I don't even bother. *Cleaning tools?*

"Yes, Alice." Edith glares at me. "You were homeless. You were mad. You thought you came from Wonderland. You told us about that stupid circus. And we made fun of you as a kid. And guess what, you were also the maid!"

Both of them laugh at me again.

"That's why you loved your buckets, soaps, and brooms." Lorina's voice is sour, but challenging. "Along with your crazy Alice books. You came to us in that dress you wore. Mum wanted to make you one of our sisters, but we insisted you stay the maid you probably were from wherever you came from. Mary Ann the maid."

Tears stream down my cheeks, but I try to forget about them. Because my childhood couldn't have been such a wreck. My existence, mad or not, must have a reason. A noble cause.

I kneel down and look for that damn thing in the buckets.

What is it? *Please make it something that brings back some of my dignity, my sanity.*

And there it is, right in front of me.

I knew it.

I knew that my existence in this world must have a reason.

Chapter 71

Alice Wonder's house, 7 Folly Bridge, Oxford

Time remaining: 39 minutes

I am staring at a golden key that looks exactly like the one Lewis Carroll gave me in the Tom Tower dream.

One of the six keys to Wonderland. The Six Impossible Keys.

Why I hid it here, I can't remember. All I know is that it's one of the six keys, and that as a child I hid this one here, for one reason or another. It meant the world to me, and was worth the humiliation I went through.

"What did you find?" Lorina demands.

I push her hand away.

Edith swings and misses my head as I duck an inch, or less. Time for some None Fu again.

I pull Edith's arms and swing her whole body as if she were my own baseball bat against the wall. She sticks like a fat piece of fresh meat for a moment, her eyes rolling back, then slides down into my buckets.

Lorina surprises me with a kick in the back.

"Take this, $%$#@!" she shouts.

I find my body plastered against the wall. She kicks me once again in my lower back and I drop to my knees, drooling.

How come this Barbie doll is that strong?

When I turn to face her, I see she has unfolded her fan

again. For the first time I notice how edgy it is. It could cut like a knife.

She throws it at me; it swirls and slices through the air before it reaches me, neck level.

I find myself catching it with a firm grip, right at a spot without blades.

"Learned a lot in your None Fu training, huh," Lorina says.

I say nothing to her, but threaten to throw the fan back at her while running in her direction. Lorina thinks I am going to try to cut her with the fan's blades, but I am not a killer. I won't stain my hands with the blood of scumbag bullies.

I keep treading with fiery eyes, happy to see the horror in hers. I keep pushing her until she falls backward into the cage through the opening where they wanted to trap me a while ago.

I watch her trip backward and lock her inside.

"How does it feel standing inside the circus now?" I say. "How does it feel to be the clown?"

Lorina starts pleading and playing good sister with me, like last time. Thankfully, I have learned my lesson. I won't be fooled.

I stare at the key in my palm and smile. Now I have two keys. I think this is my real journey. To collect the Six Impossible Keys to Wonderland—for what reasons, or cause, I have no idea.

But just when I think I have it all under control, I sense someone standing behind me. I turn to face them, thinking it will be Edith.

But it's not.

It's a man with a long hat, and teacups dangling from his black tuxedo.

Chapter 73

Alice Wonder's house, 7 Folly Bridge, Oxford

Time remaining: 22 minutes

“I’ve been waiting for this moment,” the Hatter says, although I can’t see his face—he wears a funny mask. Not so funny, really, since it’s a clown’s mask.

“Why show yourself now?” I grip my key harder, feeling it has to do something with it.

“Because you did like I planned,” he says. “To the letter.”

“I don’t understand,” I say. “You made me think I am chasing a rabbit, leading from place to place, so I could remember my past. What’s in it for you?”

“A lot,” he says. “But first let’s look into what happened. They call it the Rabbit Hole, a scientific term, I believe?”

The memory of me sitting in the psychiatry office in the asylum returns. That man in the dark with the smoking pipe telling me I am insane, that I am just a crippled girl living in my own imagination to escape the horrors that happened to me.

I remember he did tell me about the Rabbit Hole, one of the methods to push a patient’s imagination with their backs against the wall until they remembered what they were trying to forget.

“I had to go through all these puzzles, so I can tickle your memory,” the Hatter says. “You’d been in the asylum for so long and hadn’t remembered anything yet, Alice. Time was running out, and I needed you to at least remember one part of your past.

A part that interests me the most."

"My childhood?" I ask.

He says nothing. I think his clown mask is trying to forge a smile. A dark one.

"Ah," I say. "I get it. You weren't after my memories. Not really. You were after..."

"This." He pulls my hand and snatches the key from it in one move. "The first key in six, so I can open the doors to Wonderland again."

How foolish am I? Really!

"I don't care about you at all," the Hatter says. "I only care about the keys, which I believe Carroll hid with you, and then you hid them in separate places in this real world. Let's say it wasn't hard getting this one."

I realize this Hatter is much stronger than me. I can't get this key back. But I also realize he doesn't know Lewis gave me a key before, in the Tom Tower dream. So, if it's any consolation, and even if he finds the next four keys, I will always have one he doesn't know exists.

"I am going to leave now," he says. "Thank you for your cooperation."

"What makes you think I won't stop you?" I step forward.

"Because you still have a rabbit to catch." He grins. "Haven't you seen the TV? The world is in a panic because of a tiny rabbit."

"Because you made them, and me, think there is a bomb

inside."

"Who said that isn't true?" He pulls off his hat and then a rabbit from underneath, the one ticking with the bomb. "Please take it," he says. "Figure a way to stop the bomb. You have about eighteen minutes to do that."

I hug the rabbit in my arms and pat it gently. Poor thing, pushed into a mad world of Wonderlanders.

"And by the way," the Hatter says. "I wanted to make this as exciting a finale as possible, so I called the police. They are surrounding the house. People are out there everywhere. They all demand the rabbit be killed—choked, or drowned in the river to get rid of the bomb."

"Why would you do that?" My mouth is agape.

"Why wouldn't I? What's the point of life if there isn't enough madness?" he says. "See you later, Alice. For now, you're stuck between exploding with the poor rabbit in your arms or giving it away to the people outside so they can kill it themselves. Talk about a paradox."

Chapter 74

Alice Wonder's house, 7 Folly Bridge, Oxford

Time remaining: 14 minutes

Outside, the police point their guns at me.

Everywhere around me there is some kind of microphone or a news reporter. Behind them, hordes of people boo at me.

"Get rid of the rabbit!"

"Kill it!"

"She is the one who let the rabbit loose!"

Slowly, I step forward as the police demand I hand them the rabbit.

"Do you have a bomb expert who may know how to defuse the bomb?" I ask politely, well aware my maid's dress and the blood on my face isn't really helping my image.

"We don't need a bomb squad," says the lanky officer I saw in the Six O'clock Circus. "We'll drown it in the river and let it explode in there."

"But what about the rabbit?"

"You're not going to pull that 'animal rights' crap on us again, are you?" another officer says. "We know who you are, you and that imposter, Professor Carter Pillar. You've both escaped the asylum."

"She is mad!" an old woman yells from the crowd.

Like always, I wonder who is mad here. Am I such a silly,

unreasonable girl because I want to save a rabbit as much as I want to save myself?

"Hand me the rabbit, Alice," a familiar voice says. It's Inspector Dormouse, wide awake now. "I know who you are now. We got the memo. Let's make this easier on everyone. Hand the rabbit over and let us escort you back to the asylum. You're not well, young lady."

I don't move, patting the scared rabbit and hugging it closer to my chest. I can feel its escalating heartbeat.

For a moment, I realize the scope of what I have been through for two days. This Hatter, not only did he push me to remember the circus to get to the key, he also managed to raise my uneasiness with the world around me. Looking at the police, the reporters, and the crowd, I can't overlook the fact that they are the descendants of those who created the circus and used the mentally ill as a form of entertainment.

The idea confuses me.

Am I supposed to take the Wonderland Monsters' side? If not, then give me one reason why I should keep saving a human life every day.

"Pillar!" I shout. "Where are you?"

It's funny, yet sad, how he is always my last resort. With all the madness surrounding me, I prefer *his* madness the most.

"The Pillar has been sent back to the asylum, Alice," Inspector Dormouse tells me. "He can't help you. Give back the rabbit. I think you only have three minutes left. Give it to us and we'll drown it in the river. And we'll all be safe."

The world is such a useless place, that's all I can think of now. It's full of hypocrites, liars, and selfish people. And even if I'm dramatizing things, I realize I prefer to go back to the asylum. At least I know who is who in there.

But first, and since I am a mad girl on national TV, I need to do one last crazy thing.

I run through the cops with the rabbit in my arms, neglecting all the panic and shouting around me. I run away with the rabbit, which I am not going to hand over or drown in the water.

I don't know what will happen to both of us. But I feel we're both the same in this world. We're both overwhelmed by human cruelty—and stupidity—in this mad world. I hug tighter and run away with it.

And before I know it, I hear the explosion.

Chapter 75

Buckingham Palace, London

"Hoooraaay!"

Tom Truckle was overwhelmed by the hailing crowd staring at the screen. They all stood up, clinking glasses and smiling and congratulating each other, as if celebrating an independence day.

Tom stood up, pretending to be as enthusiastic, unable to believe what he'd just seen.

Did he just watch Alice Wonder explode with that rabbit on live TV?

It seemed like it.

And it seemed normal, in a very abnormal way, to have all those lunatic guests of the Queen hail the explosion and the madness it caused. But why were people in the streets happy about Alice's explosion?

Families congratulated each other and let out sighs of relief, as did the police officers and reporters. It seemed like Alice's death was the best thing that had happened to them in their lives. Everyone was happy the bomb went off on the poor mad girl who'd just escaped the asylum. As long as it didn't hurt them, it was just okay.

"And this, my fellow loons"—the Queen of England snickered in the microphone—"is just a small example of the kinds of madness we'll bestow on this world we live in."

Was that the plan? To drive the world mad, really?

"Enjoy this hilarious scene for a while," the Queen said. "And then I will tell you about the ultimate plan. I will tell you about the real Wonderland Wars!" she said as if she were Hitler, brought back from the grave and wearing a wig.

Chapter 76

Psychiatry, Radcliffe Lunatic Asylum

I am back were it all started, in that awful dark room with that awful doctor. I am lying on the couch, and my leg feels numb.

"So that's all that happened?" he asks.

"More or less," I reply. "It was a hectic adventure. The most nonsensical of all."

"And how did you survive the explosion?"

"It turned out the Pillar managed to escape his cell—of course, since when could anyone keep him locked inside?" I say. "He created this hoax of an explosion to drive people away from me, and also to give them what they wanted. A relief that it was all over."

"And the rabbit?"

"It didn't explode. This whole rabbit bomb was a hoax, too. The Hatter made it swallow a flashing device to fool me."

"So all he really wanted from you was the key," he says, skeptically, as usual.

"I believe so," I say. "He also wanted to mess with my head for some reason."

"Do you have any idea what the key will do?"

"I suppose it's one of six keys to go back to Wonderland." I don't tell him I have a key in my cell. I don't trust him that much.

“Hmm...” I hear him write something down.

“Hmm... what?”

“Nothing,” he says. “I think your condition is worsening, Alice. I mean, look at your story. It doesn’t make sense. It doesn’t even have a context. It’s contradictory. And yet you have not come back to your senses.”

“Madness doesn’t make sense. And it’s contradictory.”

“So you finally admit your madness?”

“Not *that* madness,” I say. “The other madness.”

“There are two kinds of madness now?” He really doesn’t like this conversation.

“Yes, of course. There is that loony-toony bonkers madness where you’re wrapped up in a straitjacket and locked inside a room.”

“And the other madness?”

“It’s all out there in the world you live in, doctor,” I say. “I mean, you may think it’s not madness, only because you’re used to it. But it surely is all messed up.”

“Uh-huh.” He takes a deep breath. “Look, Alice. I have no idea where to take the therapy from here. All I know is that I will prescribe you more Lullaby pills, and, sorry to say, this time I prefer you go back to the Mush Room. A few shock sessions might stir some sort of progress.”

I purse my lips for a while, contemplating if the shock therapy still scares me. I think it doesn’t. It’s just pain. And trust me, there are much worse things in this life than pain. “Tell me, doctor," I say, "do you at least believe what I said about the circus, the Invisible Plague?"

"I know for a fact it's real," he says. "Sadly, many mentally ill have been wrongfully treated in the past. What I don't believe is that you time-traveled to witness it with your own eyes, let alone the patients were all Wonderlanders."

"But let's say you believe," I say. "What would you do? I mean, would you take the people's side or the mentally ill's side?"

The doctor stays silent for a long time, then he says something that shocks me: "To a degree, we're all mentally ill, Alice. It's just that on a scale of one to ten, you're infinity in your illness. Infinity means straitjacket in an isolated cell."

Chapter 77

Alice's cell, Radcliffe Lunatic Asylum

I can't take my eyes off Waltraud as she ushers me into my cell. I want to tell her that I saw her in the circus, but I am sure she will deny it, and then I wouldn't know where to take the conversation from there.

I watch her lock me up. Today she says nothing. She doesn't mock or make fun of me. I wonder why.

"Rest the night," she says. "Tomorrow, you're first on my shock therapy list. And you know how good of a customer you are to me."

"I know," I say behind bars. "I assume I am as good as those you tortured in the circus?"

She takes a moment to look at me, but she doesn't seem to grasp any of it. "I guess that's one of your loony stories again. A circus? Is that part of the *Alice Underground* book?"

"Nah." I wave it off. "It's nothing."

I could ask her if she saw me on the news, running away with a rabbit in my hand, but I know she usually denies I was on the news.

I watch her walk away, and sit down next to my Tiger Lily. It's weird how I feel at home. I am sorry, but I really missed my cell.

Chapter 78

Alice's cell, Radcliffe Lunatic Asylum

Sometime around midnight, I hear a knock on my door. I stand up and stare at whoever it is behind the bars. I am sure I won't panic if it turns out to be the Cheshire disguised as Ogier again. I have seen my share of spooks lately.

But it's not the Cheshire. It's Margaret Kent.

"I am not dreaming, am I?" I say to her.

"Nor are you hallucinating," she says, wearing her expensive jewelry and dress.

"That's hard to swallow," I reply. "Because why in the world would you visit me, Duchess?"

"It's an unofficial visit, Alice—or whoever you really are." She chews on the words. It's apparent that she is disgusted by the asylum. "I have a message for you."

"From whom?"

"From the Queen of England."

"Her majesty?" I say it in an ironic way, still wondering if this is really happening.

"We have the key, Alice," Margaret says in a sharp businesswoman tone. "The Hatter works for us. We planned it all. The rabbit. The bomb. Everything. We had to push you to the edge of your mind so you would remember where you hid the key—one of the six, to be precise."

I'm not that surprised. In fact, the more pieces of the puzzle that come together, the better I feel. "When you say 'we,' you mean who exactly?"

"Black Chess," she says. "The Wonderlanders who were tortured by humans in the Circus. No one can't stop us."

"But not all Wonderlanders are on Black Chess's side."

"I know what the March Hare told you," she says. "You know how we know? Because the light bulb in his head is real. We can see through his thoughts. He tried to protect in you by not tell you everything because he knew we'll know. The light bulb is a Lewis Carroll invention."

"I don't care how powerful you are," I say. "Fabiola showed you which side I'm really on."

"So we're playing with open cards right now?" she laughs. "Funny you mention cards." She smirks. "Now that you don't even have Jack in your life."

This gets on my nerves. It hurts so much I want to puke my guts out. Damn the Duchess.

"Look, I don't have much time, and like I said, I have a message for you," she says. "I know you still have so many questions—hell, *I* have so many questions. But the bottom line is this. The Wonderland Wars are partially about the Six Impossible Keys Lewis gave you in the past. Don't ask me why they are important. You will know in time."

"I figured out that much about the keys, and I figured I don't remember where I hid them, and that you'll do your best to make me remember to get to them," I say. "So tell me what you're really here for."

"Let me put it this way," she says. "Although you found the key, you didn't really remember where you hid it. Hell, you didn't even remember the circus in Wonderland happened. From what the Hatter told me, you only remembered what your sisters did to you in real life."

"So?"

"So, as much as you seem to know about Alice, we're not sure you're her yet, but..." She jabs a finger in the air. "The Queen wants you on our side."

"Are you offering a position in Black Chess, really?" I snort.

"Think about it. You'll be a free girl. We'll get you out of the asylum. You won't have to struggle with Wonderland Monsters each week. What else can you ask for?"

"And you expect me to lead you to the keys, of course."

"There is a price to everything, and sanity is almost priceless."

"You're dreaming, Duchess," I say. "Whether I am Alice or not, the fact that deep in my memory I know where the keys are obliges me to hold on to them." I can't forget how concerned Lewis was about the key he gave me in the Tom Tower. "Besides, tell me one logical reason why I would want to be on the Queen's side in this war."

"You want a reason?" Margaret smirks again. She nears the bars and stares into my eyes. "I have one good reason for you, especially if you turn out to be the Real Alice."

"And what could that be?" I challenge her.

Her answer comes like a heavy tide threatening to swallow me into a sea of sharks. "Because you may not remember it yet, but you were one of us inside the cage in the circus. What humans have done to us was done to you, just the same." Even though I don't remember that, it bothers me dearly. "Haven't you noticed how most people in this world are never on your side? Haven't you noticed how they were happy thinking you died with the rabbit today? You're one of us, Alice. You just don't know it yet."

Chapter 79

Buckingham Palace, London

Tom Truckle was listening to the Queen's plan.

"All of you, my dear guests, lunatics, and ex-Wonderlanders, come from so many countries around the world," she began. "All of you are friends with presidents and the most prestigious men and women in your land. And all of you don't like any of them, too, because all of you were once in the circus."

Tom kept listening.

"Having managed to escape Wonderland and faking a new life in this awful world doesn't mean you don't want to have your revenge," she said. "Trust me, if you don't let the madness out, you'll end up like the Muffin Man, confused, not knowing who he is, and then die miserably."

Tom was beginning to see where this was going.

"My plan is simple," she said. "To get you to replace your human superiors, to replace your presidents, and to rule instead."

A long silence fell on the room.

"Think about it." She eyed everyone. "What good has any human done to the world? All this poverty, war, and—ahem—madness they caused. Humans think they can rule, but they're just jub jubs, doing a lousy job. It's time for us to rule this world." She raised her hands in the air, the tension rising in the meeting hall. "It's time for us to spread the madness!"

Tom shared the claps and enthusiasm of the crowd. He felt silly, but he also felt he needed it.

"And we're not going to try to make a better job of what the failed humans did," she elaborated. "We'll make it worse. We'll make the poor become poorer."

"Yeah!"

"The rich become filthy freakin' richer!"

"Yeah."

"We're going to turn humans into second-class citizens, if not animals."

"Yeah!"

"We, Wonderlanders, are going to rule the world!"

"Yeah!" hailed Tom. How he wished he was really part of this revolution of madness.

"And to start the Wonderland Wars," she said, "we're going to spread our insanity bit by bit, until no insane person is locked away anymore."

Tom clapped like everyone else. He realized that he might be as mad as everyone else. Maybe he wasn't destined to direct an asylum. Maybe he was destined to be one of the great Wonderlanders.

He pulled out his bottle and spilled the pills on the floor. He didn't need them anymore. He didn't need to suppress his madness and hide from everyone. Instead, he needed to celebrate it like the Queen of Hearts did.

With anticipation, he awaited what was going to happen to

the world in the coming days.

Chapter 80

Two days later,

the Pillar's cell, Radcliffe Lunatic Asylum

"You're all I have in this world," I tell the Pillar, having asked Dr. Truckle for permission to visit him.

"I wouldn't count on that," he says, smoking his hookah. "At some point, I will leave you in all this mess, Alice. I am just guiding you until you find your purpose."

"Fair enough. I don't like you that much anyways," I tease him.

"Never liked me that much, too." He rolls his eyes. "So did you make up your mind, whether you're one of them or against them?"

"I'm on Lewis' team all the way," I say. "I saw them in the dream. Lewis, Fabiola, that mysterious girl, Jack, and the March Hare. I am going to find them all and gather them to face Black Chess before they mess up this beautiful world."

"Beautiful?" The Pillar raises an eyebrow. "I thought it was a mad world."

"Mad is beautiful," I say. "It has its flaws, but when shared with the good-hearted it's beautiful."

"So you're going to continue to save lives next week?"

"Like I did this week," I say. "I know you think it's just a rabbit, but I am very okay with having saved one."

"Rabbits are cute." He took a drag from his hookah. "Just

stop following them into their holes."

I let out a light laugh. "You're definitely right about that."

"Did Margaret tell you about who this Hatter may be?"

"Nah. She just made her offer and I refused."

"And you're sure you don't have grudges against people, having been put in the circus with the others in the past?"

"First of all, I am not sure that happened. Second, there is no point in holding grudges. Some people kill and do horrible things; other people are most lovable in this world. I need to learn how to tune my inner compass to find the good ones."

"That's poetic."

"How about you, Pillar?"

"What about me?"

"Where you in the circus as well?" It's an important question to me. I wonder if I'll ever understand his motives.

"I was." He nods, but he seems wary about talking about it. I wonder what they did to him. "I am surprised you didn't see me in your dream—or whatever that Wonderland portal was. Which reminds me, do you still have that Wonderland map on your phone?"

"Nah, it stopped working when I woke up," I say. "Why? Looking for something?"

"It's just that there was this store that sold music in Wonderland."

"What about it?"

"Instead of selling CDs they sold flamingos that

memorized every tune in a certain album," he says. "So you go pay for the latest Taylor Swift album and they give you a flamingo..."

"Who sings all the Taylor Swift songs." I laugh. "That's bonkers. But you still can buy any song here in real life."

"That one song I am looking for, you can only find in Wonderland."

"Really? What's it called?"

"'What if God Was Mad Like Us, Just a Nut Like Most of Us.'"

Chapter 81

Alice's cell, Radcliffe Lunatic Asylum

Back in my cell I sit next to my silent Tiger Lily and enjoy the silence. There is this strange feeling that follows every episode of madness I encounter; it's that euphoric feeling of: *I'm great. I managed to survive another day in this insane world.*

What a great feeling.

I plan to sleep today, continue my Mush Room sessions with Waltraud tomorrow, then wait for a new mission around next week. Let's step it up a notch, Queen of Hearts!

For my own sanity, and safety, I make sure Lewis' key is still hidden in the wall of the cell. It is, and it should stay safe in here.

I have no idea how I will get the next one, or if I will be able to get back the one with the Queen of Hearts now, but we'll see what happens.

To put myself to sleep, I sing, "*I am mad, mad girl in a mad, mad world, it's not a bad, bad thing if I am crazy.*"

But suddenly, I hear someone sing it in the cell next to me. It's not a girl's voice but a boy's.

I keep singing, and that boy sings with me.

Slowly it dawns on me. "Jack?" I whisper to the wall.

"Who else do you think is mad enough about you he'd voluntarily go in an asylum to be with you?" he says from behind the wall.

I place my two palms on the wall, wanting to hug it, and maybe kiss it. I can't believe this is true.

"Jack," I pant. "How did you make it? I thought you were crossing over to the other side."

"Let's put it this way," he says in a smiley voice, "I told the guys in the hell to go to hell."

"Poetic." I laugh.

"I also told them I'm mad about you, so they suggested I came here," he says. "They didn't think I'd do it."

"But I don't think anyone can voluntarily come to the asylum. I mean, it's ironic that if you tell someone you're mad, they probably won't believe you."

"Not until you walk butt naked across the street in front of them," Jack chirps.

I laugh hysterically.

Then the evil thought hits me that I may be just imagining it.

I turn around and watch my Tiger Lily. She is just standing still. She isn't talking to me, so Jack must be real.

"I missed you so much, Jack," I tell him.

"Me too," he says. "How about we go on a date tomorrow?"

"Date? Where?"

"I managed to slip my name to Waltraud," he says. "So I'm right behind you in the Mush Room list. Not a bad place to meet."

I am floored. Laughing. Happier than ever. I love this goofy and weird guy. He just wants to be with me. What else can I ask for?

"It's a mad world, Alice," he says. "But together, we…"

"Together we can make it through." I cut in.

"And you know how we'll do it?"

"Have no clue," I chuckle."

"By being madder."

I almost cry out of joy. With all things not making sense, Jack here next to me make the most sense of all.

And even if I am imagining him, I don't mind. I love you, Jack Diamond, and together we're about to stand up against Black Chess in the most nonsensical—but greatest—war of all time.

Epilogue

Director's office, Radcliffe Lunatic Asylum

Dr. Tom Truckle, still sipping his favorite mock turtle soup, was watching the Pillar with intent through the surveillance camera.

The Pillar was smoking his hookah as usual. He was wiggling his feet and singing along to a song called "What if God Was Mad Like Us." Tom actually liked the tune.

What was new? The Pillar was happy as usual, not giving a damn about this world.

But Tom was still puzzled, staring at the invitation he'd received from the Queen to attend the Event.

The invitation that hadn't been for him.

The invitation that had originally been to professor Carter Cocoon Chrysalis Pillar.

Why had the Queen of England invited the Pillar to the Event? That puzzled Tom a lot.

He wished he could figure it out, watching the Pillar in his cell twenty-four-seven. But the Pillar never did anything strange or hinting to a clue.

Until now...

Dr. Tom Truckle watched the Pillar stand up and pull out a secret drawer in his favorite couch. From inside, he pulled out a mask of a clown, then he pulled out a long leather coat, and lastly a ridiculously long hat.

That among a number of teacups.

Tom squinted, horror filling his eyes. This couldn't be. This just couldn't be.

The Pillar sat back on the couch, smoking his hookah and staring at something his hand. Something Tom couldn't see without zooming in.

Tom zoomed in, and he could see it.

While the Pillar was humming "What if God Was Mad Like Us," he was holding a golden key in his hand. He kept staring it with a wide smirk from ear to ear on his face, fiddling with the key and smoking his hookah.

The END...

Alice will return in Hookah (Insanity 4)

Thank You

Thank you for purchasing and downloading this insane book (probably three of them at this point—big grin). I'm so happy, and grateful, to be able to share this story with you, and I hope you enjoyed reading it as much as I enjoyed making it up!

Talking about making things up, not everything is a figment of my imagination. All locations, including *Ha Ha Street*, and *Piccadilly Circus* with its *Statue* and *Arrow*, and the incredibly mysterious *Garden of Cosmic Speculation*, are real (and yes, part of it was modeled after Wonderland, and the public can only access it one day per year, but it doesn't belong to the March Hare, of course). Maybe you'll have the chance to visit them someday.

The historical facts about the *Circus* and the *Invisible Plague* are sadly true. But in order to not spoil the next book, I'd prefer to elaborate on them later.

And, of course, all the tidbits from Lewis Carroll's Wonderland riddles are straight from the book, although I have added a few of my own interpretations.

But make no mistake; *Zashchishchaiushchikhsya* is a real Russian word, which Lewis Carroll was fascinated by in his one and only trip out of England.

I've also created a special Pinterest page for you, where you can see for yourself all the places and riddles Alice and Pillar visited—and a few images of the Invisible Plague, the Garden in

Scotland, and a few other interests.

Hookah (Insanity 4) will be released soon, so please stay tuned to my Facebook Page:

http://Facebook.com/camjace

or

http://cameronjace.com for more information.

If you have a question, please message me on Facebook; I love connecting with all of my readers, because without you, none of this would be possible. http://cameronjace.com

Thank you, for everything.

Like I said, I'm delaying every detail until the next book to avoid spoilers. But I'd to address the beautiful people of Britain and apologize if I got a wrong fact here and there. I'm not English but it's been a pleasure delving into Lewis Carroll's masterpiece and hunting its roots all over London, Oxford, and his hometown. A mysteriously beautiful country, indeed.

And wow, it's been more than two years since I first published my first book, and how lucky I was that all you believed in that story—and me. I am forever in debt.

Thanks again for being mad.

Cameron.

Subscribe to Cameron's Mailing List

To receive exclusive updates from Cameron Jace and to be the first to get your hands on Hookah: Insanity 4, please sign up to be on his personal mailing list!

You'll get instant access to cover releases, chapter previews and the only readers to be eligible to win prices!

Www.cameronjace.com

About the Author

Cameron Jace is the boy next door who managed, by some miracle, to be come the bestselling author of the Grimm Diaries series and the Insanity series. A graduate of the College of Architecture, and a devout collector of out-of-print books, he is obsessed with the origins of folk tales and the mysterious storytellers who first told them. Three of his books made Amazon's Top 100 Customer Favorites in Kindle 2013 and Amazon's Top 100 kindle list. Cameron lives in California with his girlfriend. When he isn't writing or collecting books, he is reading or playing his guitar.

41856736R00157

Made in the USA
San Bernardino, CA
21 November 2016